T0381000

Millie

Jesse Ward

authorHOUSE

AuthorHouse™
1663 Liberty Drive
Bloomington, IN 47403
www.authorhouse.com
Phone: 833-262-8899

Published by AuthorHouse 08/14/2023

ISBN: 979-8-8230-1329-1 (sc)
ISBN: 979-8-8230-1330-7 (hc)
ISBN: 979-8-8230-1328-4 (e)

Library of Congress Control Number: 2023915214

Print information available on the last page.

This book is printed on acid-free paper.

Because of the dynamic nature of the Internet, any web addresses or links contained in this book may have changed since publication and may no longer be valid. The views expressed in this work are solely those of the author and do not necessarily reflect the views of the publisher, and the publisher hereby disclaims any responsibility for them.

Prologue

Doctor Weber,

Thank you for the last several days. During that time, you have been very kind to me, but I have not been kind to you. I have deceived you. You have no idea who I am. If you have feelings for me, you have feelings for a person who does not exist. If we should ever meet again, I would hope that you would have feelings for me, and not the person I pretended to be while I was here. I am going back to the United States to wait for my husband and hope that he will forgive me and love me for who I am. I know that last night you told me information that you want to keep private. You can rest assured that I will keep your secret safe.

Bobbi

Millie

The war to end all wars ended in the fall of 1918. Two things were certain about the end of the war. One, it was not a war to end all wars, and it created a very unstable time in Europe. Millie Berenson was born in the fall of 1918 two months before the end of the so-called Great War. It was not the best of times to be Jewish, but growing up in a Post War era, Millie was unaware of this. She was just a smart little girl from a loving family who was just like the rest of the people in her community in Munich. Millie had an older brother, Benjamin, three years her senior who was everything a big brother should be. He was proud of his little sister, and they were close. When Millie entered school, she had no idea of the hate that was boiling underneath the social and political climate of Germany. It was just waiting to come to the surface.

During the 1920s, times were hard for most of the people of Germany. The war had destroyed the economy. Germany had lost the war, and most of the people did not understand why. They had lost no battles on their home soil. They did not understand why the Allied powers had made them take the blame for the war. The German people did not feel that they had started the war, but were victims of the imperial ambitions of the major countries of Europe.

Political parties sprang up, and they were looking for someone to blame for the loss of the war. The same people who had applauded the fall of the royal families, welcomed parliamentary democratic reform, and rejoiced at the armistice, were now blaming the left, Socialists, Communists, and Jews for losing the war. They called this Dolchstosslegende (stab-in-the-back). All people were struggling, but Millie's mother and father made a decent living with a store. It was a large general store, and it sold a variety of goods. Millie as a young child did not seem to notice or care that she was Jewish, and her family seemed to be accepted. This would change during the 1930s.

Millie's education was a mixture of public schooling and home school. When she was nine years old, she became aware of Hitler, and even though Hitler was spouting anti-Jewish rhetoric, nothing affected her lifestyle. She was fifteen years old when Hitler became head of the German government. It was at this time that she began to see the changes in the people of Germany toward the Jewish people.

Millie finished school in 1934, and things in Germany were becoming life-threatening for the Jews. Starting in mid-1933, the Nazi regime started passing laws and decrees that eroded the rights of Jews in Germany. It was then that her father became worried for his family. Millie wanted to become a doctor and was making plans. One night he asked for Millie and her mother to join him in the study.

"Millie, your mother, and I know you want to go to medical school and that you have applied and been accepted in Switzerland. I know you are still waiting to hear from Berlin. We think you should go to Switzerland. I have written to my sister, and she has agreed for you to live with them while you complete your education."

Millie was caught off guard. "I might get some aid if I go to Berlin. I would not be able to get any help if I go to Switzerland. Besides, if I go to Switzerland, I will be so far from you and Mother."

"That is the whole point. It is not safe here anymore. You cannot live here and go to medical school. If you think a Jew is going to get aid, you are dreaming. You do not have to worry about the money. We are okay. We put some money aside before the war."

Millie persisted in her argument. "But what about you and Mother and Benjamin? If it is not safe for me, how are you going to be safe?"

"We plan to sell the store and leave. We hope we can do it soon, but we cannot leave until we sell the store. Benjamin is going to help me run the store until we sell it. Be packed and ready to go. We will leave in about a week."

Several days later, Millie and her father left Bavaria and drove to Switzerland. When they got to his sister's home, Jakob and Margaret were delighted to see them, and they made Millie feel at home.

The next day, her father drove to Zurich. When he returned, he sat at the kitchen table and said, "I have set up a bank account in the bank at Zurich. It is in my name and Millie's. Millie, you will have to sign this card and mail it to the bank."

Turning to his brother-in-law, he said, "Jakob, I have a check that should cover the cost of Millie going to school. You can pay for Millie's educational expenses and other things she might need. If she should need more, just contact me and let me know. The account I have set up is for us to leave Germany if things go bad. We are leaving as soon as I can sell the store."

The next morning, he hugged his daughter and drove away.

Two weeks later, Millie was taking her first class. It was not long until Millie felt at home living with her aunt and uncle. She did feel guilty about leaving her mother, father, and brother.

Millie liked going to school, and time passed quickly for her. During the last several months of 1937, Millie wrote and received a letter every week from her parents. Her mother, who wrote the letters, never mentioned how bad things were getting in Germany. She also never mentioned how selling the store was going.

Millie became consumed with her education. She was always at the top or near the top of her classes.

By 1938, the letters from her parents became further apart, and Millie assumed things were not going well for them.

Kristallnacht (Night of the Broken Glass) occurred on November 9th and 10th in 1938. *Kristallnacht* changed the nature of Nazi Germany's persecution of the Jews from economic, political, and social exclusion to physical violence, including beatings, incarceration, and murder; the event is often referred to as the beginning of the Holocaust. Millie was frightened for her parents and brother. She wanted to rejoin them, but her uncle, fearing for her safety, would not let her go.

"I am not so sure you could get back to Munich safely, and your parents would never forgive me if I let you go."

"Why has this occurred? Why have I not heard from Mom and Dad?"

"I don't know why we have not heard from your father and mother. Jewish businesses have been attacked all over Germany. Even if your parents wanted to contact us, I do not think they could. I do know why

3

this occurred. It is because a Jewish student shot and killed Ernst vom Rath, a German diplomat, in Paris."

She did not understand. The truth was her parents were not okay. All the windows of their store were destroyed and had to be covered with plywood panels. When she received a letter from her mother, she said there was only light damage to the store, and they planned to leave Germany soon, even if they could not sell the store. Millie felt better knowing that they were all right.

Soon did not come, and soon the letters stopped coming altogether.

By the early spring of 1942, Millie was a doctor needing just to finish her residence requirement, but it had been more than three years since she had heard from her parents or her brother. She had two concerns. The British and Americans were bombing deep inside Germany and there was a chance her home would be destroyed because she knew there was a synthetic rubber plant nearby. The news about what was happening to the Jews was frightening. She tried to dismiss the idea that her parents and brother were in a Jewish prison camp or even dead.

While she was attending school, she met a young man who worked for his parents at a local printing shop. His name was Frank Christian. He was about her age, and they saw each other from time to time. Millie did not have much free time, but when she did, she and Frank would go out to eat and sometimes go to the movies. Sometimes she would go to the movies without Frank because she wanted to see the newsreels. The newsreels were full of propaganda and did not show how bad things were, but the local news presented a different story about the war, and how bad it was for the Jews.

She was not sure how she felt about Frank, because as soon as the war was over, she planned to return to Germany, find her family, and start her medical career. The more news she heard the more concerned about her parents she became. Jews were being rounded up and put into camps. Like most people outside of Germany, she did not know of the Final Solution. The Final Solution was a policy of the Nazi Party, a policy of deliberate and systematic genocide formulated by Nazi leadership in January of 1942. But, in the spring of 1944, everyone knew the war for Germany was not going well. She had often told Frank about how she wanted to find out about her parents and brother. She dreamed that she could slip across the border into Germany and sneak back to Munich and see or rescue her parents and brother who she felt were now in hiding.

In April 1944, Millie's uncle came to her and told her that he needed to talk. "Your father is not a poor man. I fear that the Gestapo has arrested him, but I don't know this for sure. What you need to know, your father wrote down in this letter. Your father told me if I thought something had happened to him, I was to give you the letter. It has been nearly six years since we have heard from your parents, and I fear..." He paused and handed the letter to Millie.

Millie looked at the letter, read it slowly, and then read it again.

> *Millie, if you are reading this letter, it means that you have not heard from me or your mother for a long time. You remember that when I brought you to Switzerland, I set up a bank account. If you are reading this, it means we did not escape. The account is now yours. Once you have finished your medical education, you need to stay in Switzerland. Do not come back to Munich.*

Tears were rolling down Millie's cheeks. "Do you think that they are dead or in a prison camp?"

"I don't know." Jakob thought there was little chance that his brother-in-law was still alive, but he wanted to give Millie some hope.

With a broken voice, Millie said, "Somehow I feel that they are still alive. I must find a way to get back to Munich and find out."

Jakob looked at his niece. "We must wait. Meanwhile, we must operate like they have been killed and follow your parents' wishes. Many feel the war may end this year. Americans and the English are both bombing deep inside Germany. The news is reporting that there might be an Allied invasion."

Millie was angry. "I am not sure I can wait that long."

Jakob was calm. "I don't think you have a choice. Let's talk about your father's note to you. Do you know how much he left in the account?"

"I have relied on the money he gave you and Aunt Margaret. The money that Father gave you has been all I needed. I also know that you and Aunt Margaret have helped a lot."

"We need to go to the bank. We will need to prepare for the worst and hope for the best. There is something else. Your father left me a key. It is for a safety deposit box. There is a number on it, and we will check the box when we get to the bank."

Millie took the key and looked at it. "I don't know how much money is in the account, but I need to share it with you and Aunt Margaret."

"I don't want you to worry. We have enough money. As you see, there might be more. I suggest you leave the money in the account, and as soon as the war is over, you and I will take you home and we will see if we can find your family. Who knows, miracles do happen?"

Millie didn't say anything at first. "You fear the worst for them."

"I do. But there is nothing we can do but wait. Two things must happen before we can go into Germany. First, you must finish medical school, and second, the war must end. You have about finished your training, and the news is saying that Germany is losing to Russia on the Eastern Front. There are also rumors about a second front being opened in France. I think the war will be over by the end of the year."

Millie hugged her uncle. "I hope you are right." As she held her uncle she thought, *That is much too long to wait. If Germany is losing the war, there is no telling what Hitler will do to the Jews.*

The next day, Millie and her uncle went to the bank in Zurich. Soon Millie had access to the account.

The bank attendant handed her a sheet with the balance written on it. "Good grief." She had over 100,000 Swiss Francs. "I had no idea that we had that kind of money."

"Your grandfather was a very wealthy man. Some of that money comes from his estate. Your father must have saved the rest. I am sure he had a business account back in Munich, but I would not count on it still being there."

Later they were led to a large room, and a bank attendant took Millie's key and his own and opened a very large safety deposit box. He sat the box down on a table and left the two alone.

When they opened the box, they found four stacks of Swiss Francs, or the equivalent of thirty-seven thousand dollars in American money. There were also several stacks of stock investments.

Her uncle looked at the stock and bond certificates and said, "I don't think these have much value now, but these are all American investments. I believe after the war these could be worth much more, especially if America wins the war. I don't think your father had much faith in the German economy. He would have to have made these investments during the early 1930s, about the time Hitler was coming to power. If you want to look through the box a little more, I will meet you in the lobby. I have a box here also, and I need to make a change in the contents."

Millie waited until her uncle had left, then took out the equivalent of about two thousand dollars and put it in her purse. There were some other things in the box, some jewelry, and other stuff. She didn't take time to look at it. She had other things on her mind.

She locked the box and went to meet her uncle.

That night she wondered what she should do with the lockbox key. She wanted to keep it safe. She looked at her closet door. Feeling above the door, she found a groove in the top of the door just deep enough for her key.

A week later, she was having dinner with Frank. "Frank, this is going to sound crazy, but I want to go home. I have to know what has happened to my family."

Smiling at Millie, he said, "I know you want to find out about your mother and father, but going into Germany would be crazy. Let's just think about it."

"I have seen people come and go across the border. Why can't we?"

"Once you get on the train and cross the border, the train stops on the German side. Everyone must have the proper papers. If you don't, you are arrested."

"Do these people who are going into Germany have the proper papers?"

"Most do, but some are forged."

Millie persisted, "How do you get forged papers?"

Frank did not say anything at first. Then he leaned close to Millie and said in a very low voice, "What I am going to tell you, you can't tell anyone else. Do you understand?"

Millie shook her head in the affirmative.

"I have helped my father create some of these documents."

"So, you could make papers for me."

"Yes, I can, but if you went into Germany, you would need help. Going by train would be too risky. Half the time, it is shut down because of air attacks. I know two brothers, Lars and Abe. I could contact them and see if they could meet us and drive us to Munich. It would take money. Do you have any money?"

"How much would we need?"

"They would want at least eight hundred francs. And we would need that much or more to bribe officials in Germany. Can you come up with that kind of money?"

"Yes, I have a couple of thousand in Swiss Francs. Does that mean that you would be willing to go with me?"

"It does. If you are serious about going inside Germany, get the money together, and then give me a few days to create some of the necessary documents."

A week later Frank contacted Millie and told her that everything was in place. She gave him the money and he gave her the false papers.

"Don't let anyone see these. Be ready to leave in a week."

"We will have to cross the border on foot. It will be about a five-mile walk down the mountain, and there we will meet the two brothers. They will drive us the rest of the way. Once we meet them, we will have to follow their directions."

The next week passed slowly. Millie wondered why Frank was willing to go with her. Did he care that much about her? How did he know the two brothers? Why were he and his father creating fake documents? Maybe she should wait until the war came to an end. She had the feeling that something was not right, but she was going to take the chance anyway.

The Webers

Herman Weber came to America in 1883. Herman was able to slip out of Bavaria with a good portion of his family's wealth in the form of priceless jewelry and gems, and a keen sense of business. He settled in New York and quickly mastered English. By the 1890's he had a string of businesses around the New York area.

In 1892, he met Ally Cody. She was the daughter of Andrew Cody, who had made a fortune in the railroads. Ally had graduated from college, and she had studied German. She could speak the language, and it was one of the things that had brought Herman and Ally together. She was shopping for a Christmas gift for her mother when she had gone into one of the Weber stores. Herman was in the store, and when he saw her, he decided that he would wait on her himself.

With a big smile that didn't conceal his attraction to her, he said, "Welcome to my store. May I help you?"

Ally noticed Herman's accent and said, "Bist du Deutschher?"

"Ish bin Deutscher, but I need to speak English. I am getting much better."

"Your English is fine. How long have you been here?"

"I have been here for nine years. My name is Herman Weber. Welcome to my business."

"I have seen several of your stores around the city. You are doing very well. Could you show me some rings?"

He gave her a big smile. "I can't right now. I have to take a beautiful lady to lunch and then I will be glad to help you."

She returned his smile. "How do you know the lady would be willing to go to lunch with you? You know, she could be married."

"Since I came to America, I have been very lucky. I am hoping that my luck continues to hold."

During the next year, they saw each other often, and they soon fell in love and were married in 1893.

In 1894, Herman and Ally had their only child, a son who they named Alfred. During the early part of the 20th century, their businesses continued to flourish, and Alfred became a large part of running the businesses.

During World War I, the anti-German sentiment was strong because most Americans supported England, and Herman, Ally, and Alfred, decided they should keep their German background a secret. They moved to Boston and bought two houses. While in public they spoke only English, but in their homes, they spoke only German. They felt it was important to keep their heritage alive.

Alfred meet Maria, who was also a German immigrant, and in only a short time they were married. In 1918 Alfred and Maria had twins, a boy, and a girl. They named the children Nathan and Natalie.

When Nate and Natalie started school, they were fluent in both German and English. Both Nate and Natalie graduated from high school when they were sixteen.

In the 1920s, Herman Weber and his son made a fortune in the stock market, but in 1928, Herman was beginning to worry about the market. He convinced Alfred that they should pull out. While many lost their fortune on Black Friday, the Webers were safe.

In 1935, both Herman and Ally died, and they left a good portion of their wealth to Nate and Natalie.

While Nate and Natalie were in school, they were more than brother and sister. They were best friends. They both attended Boston College and decided to attend medical school together. In 1941, Natalie met a young man. His name was Tom Elliston. He was a few years older than she and was already working at a law firm in Boston. When the Japanese bombed Pearl Harbor and America found itself at war, both Tom and Nate thought they would be drafted. Tom was called but was classified as 4F because of a back injury he had suffered as a child. Nate waited for his call, but it didn't come until much later.

In 1942, Alfred and Maria were killed in a car accident. Nate and Natalie found that they were both rich and owned quite a bit of property.

Neither wanted to run the businesses so they sold off a great deal of the company and invested in various holdings.

In the spring of 1944, both were doctors on the staff of Boston General Hospital. Natalie and Tom were living in their mother and father's home and Nate was living in their grandparents' house. Nate and Natalie co-owned both houses and had decided for one to take ownership of one house and the other to take ownership of the other. But before they could transfer the ownership of the two houses, the war put the legal proceedings on hold.

World War II

In late June 1944, Nate was drafted into the army, and in the middle of July, he was assigned to a mobile hospital unit to support Patton's 3rd Army.

Nate had mixed feelings about the war. He felt he should do his duty, and as a doctor, he could save many American lives. On the other hand, he was scared, and he hated the idea of war. He crossed the Atlantic by ship and wondered if a German submarine would attack. It was then he decided he would stop being afraid and concentrate on his job.

When he arrived in Southern France, Nate was depressed, but his depression was soon lost in the demands of working in combat. It was not long until he gained the respect of his co-workers. What he lacked in experience he made up for in skill. By the middle of August, he was considered the best surgeon in the outfit. The hospital unit was moving fast, and he was looking forward to going to Germany. If he could find time, he would be able to see where his grandfather was from and find out more about his family. In late August he was in the interior of France. He wanted to see Paris, but Patton was pushing hard to the east. His medical unit joined Patton's army. There would be no Paris for Nate. Patton was moving fast, and no sooner than the mobile medical unit was set up it was disassembled and moved to a new location.

One day, he had just completed a thirty-hour shift and had worked on so many wounded men he lost count. Leaving the operation tent, he started toward his tent when he noticed a nurse walking toward the nurse's area. She looked up and saw him and said, "Nice job in there. There is more than one lucky soldier who should be thankful that you were their doctor today."

Nate managed a weak smile. "Thank you. I am Doctor Weber." He looked at her name tag. It was smeared with blood. "You are?"

"I know who you are. My name is Rosemary, Rosemary Harris. You will have to pardon the way I am. I am on my way to clean up. It is just a little more private there."

"You don't have to ask me for forgiveness. How long were you in there?"

"Same as you. We came on duty together. I noticed you. You were in a zone, and you concentrated solely on the task in front of you. We were working together a part of the time, and you hardly looked up. You are good at what you do."

Nate tried to not show his pride. He did not like to be bragged on. "How come I have not seen you before?"

"I just got here a few days ago. I do hope we can catch a break. We need to get these wounded men back away from the lines. Many are going to need care we can't give here." Rosemary stopped walking. "Well, this is where we part. My tent is this way."

"You take care, Rosie."

Rosemary continued to walk up the path. She simply said, "See ya."

When Nate got to his tent, he fell across his cot and quickly fell asleep. It started to rain that night and the patter of rain falling on the tent created a white noise that put Nate into a deep sleep that lasted for twelve hours. When he awoke, the rain had stopped so he walked over to the mess tent and got breakfast and coffee. Just as he sat down, Rosemary walked up and said, "May I join you?"

"Hey, Rosie. Did you have a good sleep? Please sit down."

Rosemary took her seat and took a bite of her food. Then she said, "I did. I am starved. I never knew that powdered eggs could taste so good."

Then for several minutes neither said anything. They ate in silence. When they were about halfway through their meal, Nate asked, "Where are you from?"

"I am from Toledo, Ohio, but I am not going back there after the war. My husband is from Bar Harbor, Maine. His family has a business there. He most likely will join his family business."

"I didn't know that nurses could be married."

"At the start of the war they could not. I met Jim in the spring of 1942. He was so handsome, and I was swept off my feet. I was not in the army at the time. Jim had already enlisted. He was one of those young men who signed up right after the Japanese bombed Pearl Harbor. I was working at a local hospital, and he was doing his training at a local base. Well, we met at a dance club, and as they say, the rest is history. We got married and he shipped out two weeks later. In October of that same year, they changed the rules and the army started accepting nurses who were married. So, I signed up and here I am."

"Is your husband here in Europe?"

"No. He is in Hawaii. He is in a hospital. He was wounded on some island. They won't say where. Most of what I know is that he has a severe leg wound but is recovering. I write to him about it every day. What about you? Where are you from?"

"Boston. I am not married. My best friend is my sister. She is married to a fancy lawyer. I write to her about every two weeks. I have no other family. My parents died a few years ago. They were killed in a car accident. My sister and I are twins. She is also a doctor, and she is currently at Boston General."

"Do you have any plans after the war?"

"No. I may stay in Europe for a while."

"My gosh! Why?"

"When I was drafted, all I could think about was getting back to Boston. Like my sister, I was on the staff at Boston General. Being here has changed me. Have you noticed the people here? They have done nothing to deserve what has happened. Many have lost their homes, and they struggle to have enough to eat. They don't have any health care. There is no educational system left. If I can help, I might stay. I am looking forward to getting to Germany. I don't see how they can continue to hold up. Did you see the number of bombers flying over the other day? They covered the sky as far as you could see. The civilians must be suffering beyond belief. Germany must be rebuilt after the war, and I think I might want to be a part of that."

Rosemary didn't say anything but continued to eat her breakfast. *Is he for real? All I can think about is getting back home to my husband and helping as many soldiers as possible do the same. This man is looking far beyond the war.*

During September and October, Nate and Rosemary developed a close friendship, and she became the relief from the war he needed. He found they had a lot in common. She liked to read, and he asked his sister to send books, which he shared with Rosemary.

One day they had a light shift, and they were in the mess tent having dinner when Nate said, "What are you going to do after this war?"

"I am going to have babies, lots of babies. Why do you ask?"

"I thought you might want to continue your career as a nurse or maybe become a doctor. You are very good."

"Do you know how much money a nurse makes? Jim is going to be working for his parents. They do not have a very large business."

Nate didn't even look up from his meal. "I have money. I could help."

Rosemary did not take Nate too seriously. She didn't know that Nate and his sister were millionaires. "When this war ends, just cut me a check and I will live happily ever after." They both laughed.

Things were calm during the first week of December. Nate wanted to see Natalie, but he knew he would be lucky if he got a hot Christmas dinner. He enjoyed spending time with Rosemary. They often talked about their families, and she kept him up to date on her husband's progress. During the second week of December, Rosemary received word that he had returned to the United States and would be home for Christmas.

On the 16th of December, all hell broke loose. The Third Army was ordered to turn north. The Germans had broken through the American lines in the Ardennes. The field hospital was taken down and followed behind the fighting units. Casualties were expected to be high, and they were.

The medical unit spent Christmas Day traveling, and four days after Christmas they had a temporary hospital set up. It was several miles from where most of the fighting was taking place. Teams of doctors were assigned to move close to the fighting and help get wounded men stable enough to move to the field hospital to receive more care. Nate, three other doctors, and four nurses went to a small village to help with the wounded. When the team arrived, they found the town had been bombed with no buildings left intact. Medical corpsmen were stabilizing those with less severe wounds, but many required more medical attention and had to receive surgery before they could be moved. They had two medium-sized tents. One became a makeshift operating room and the other a recovery room for the wounded until they could be moved.

The fighting was intense and close. On more than one occasion they were doing fieldwork with fighting very near the tent where they were doing operations. Once they were doing surgery in a burned-out shell of a building. At one point, Nate worked for thirty straight hours. Many times, all they could do was stop the bleeding, close wounds, and try to stabilize wounded soldiers so they could be moved back to the field hospital.

Corpsmen moved the wounded men out, and they finally got a break. Nate saw Rosemary with the other nurses talking, and he thought they were going to try to get some rest in the recovery tent. Nate found a building that was one-half gone. Using wood from the bombed-out building, he built a fire and huddled up in one corner. Suddenly he heard a noise and saw Rosemary. "Care to share your fire and nice accommodations?"

"Well, it is not the Ritz, but we have a cover over our heads and a great view out the front. I thought you and the other nurses were going to sleep in the recovery tent. Do you have anything to eat?"

Rosemary moved close to the fire. "It would be impossible to get any rest there. The other girls found an abandoned truck and made a bedroom in the back. There was just enough room for three, so I slipped away. To answer your question, I have two packs of C-rations. One of the air-borne soldiers they transferred left a pack. It had several packs of C-rations. The nurses divided them up and I have two. What about you?"

"I have a couple of packs of K-rations and a canteen full of water. I have requested to have more sent to us from the field hospital."

"I hope they send some nice fresh water and a turkey dinner. Can I have some of that water? I don't have any." Rosemary took the top from the canteen. She took a large gulp of water and said, "We are going to need more."

"This top doubles as a cup. "Pack it full of snow and put it next to the fire. We will make our own water."

Nate opened a can of K-rations and handed it to Rosemary. "Well Rosie, this is not how I expected to spend my Christmas vacation. If we get back to Paris, I will take you out and buy you a Christmas dinner."

Rosemary had a concerned look on her face. "What do you mean If we get back to Paris?"

Nate suddenly realized what he said had caused Rosemary some concern. "I mean they may not send us back to Paris."

"No, that is not what you meant. You have concerns as do I. This is the closest I have been to combat. We could always hear the artillery in the distance, but during the operations and treating the wounded today, it sounded so close. I even looked out once today and saw an explosion on the next ridge."

"I did too. I feel we are going to be okay. We are here. Let's do our job and hope we get back to France quickly. I have only one blanket. How many do you have?"

Rosemary replied. "I have two blankets. Maybe we can call for room service and ask for an extra pillow. Well, at least we will be out of the snow. So, we have three blankets. We can spread one out on the floor and use the other two to keep warm."

Nate picked up several pieces of wood and put them on the fire. "I am not going to make this too big. Some hotshot German might make us a target." Nate and Rosemary made their bed and pulled the blankets over to cover themselves.

Rosemary turned her back to Nate. In a soft voice, she said. "Do you think we should take turns standing watch?"

"No. Let the hotel personnel do that. After all, for what we are paying for this nice room, we should get some services. I am going to sleep. If the Germans find me, I am going to tell them to just shoot me. I think I might be dead anyway. Good night, Rosie."

Nate and Rosemary had been asleep for about four hours when the artillery started. Most of the shelling was close to where the American lines were, but one blast was only about two hundred yards away from where they were. Rosemary and Nate barely moved and went back to sleep.

The next morning Nate gave Rosemary a nudge and said, "We have been asleep for ten hours. Let's find our crew and see what we can do. By the way, we slept right through the New Year."

On the second week of January, the Germans had been pushed back and Nate's emergency team was relieved. The medical team moved back to the field hospital. By the 25th of January, the Battle of the Bulge was over, and Nate's medical unit was sent to Paris for two weeks of R&R. While in Paris, he was promoted to major. To celebrate, he took Rosemary out to eat. When they took their seats, the waiter opened a menu for each of them. Nate looked over at Rosemary and said, "I wish I could get you that Christmas dinner we missed when we were in the Ardennes. I guess we will have to settle for duck or lamb. I wonder how they can still have these on the menu?"

Rosemary smiled, "I have no idea. I got a letter from Jim today. Well, I got it today, but it was mailed three weeks ago. He is home. He says he is walking much better but still must use a walker when he leaves the house."

Nate knew what Rosemary was doing. She had changed the conversation from a Christmas dinner to include her husband. He could sense she had something on her mind. They had grown close, and this was her way of saying that they were friends and there could be nothing more between them.

"That is good. I understand that our armies are crossing over into Germany. In February we could be standing on German soil. I am looking forward to that. That means the war will soon be over. The Russians are pushing hard from the east. I don't know why the Germans don't go ahead and surrender. They are beaten."

Rosemary didn't want to talk about the war. "Tell me about Boston. I have never been there. You know that Boston is a short bus ride to my new home in Maine. We could visit some after the war. I really want you to meet my husband."

He noticed that she said her husband and not Jim. He knew what she was doing. "I would like that. When the war is over and before we get separated, we need to exchange addresses. You know that we might be assigned to different units."

He pointed to his collar. "I got a new rank."

"I noticed. Congratulations." She had not said anything because she knew his new rank might mean they were not going to be in the same unit anymore. She didn't want to think about losing her friend. In a low quiet voice, she said, "What are you going to do tomorrow?"

"I am going to see the sights of Paris. Do you want to join me?"

She wanted to spend more time with him, but she said, "No. I am spending time with the girls, and we will be doing the same as you. We may see you while you are out and about."

"I am going to start at the Eiffel Tower. What about your crew?"

"You know that I would love to join you. I like being with you. You once told me that your best friend was your sister. You are my best friend here, but I am not sure that is possible. I fear our co-workers may be talking about us. That is why I am joining the girls tomorrow. You are my friend and I care a great deal for you, but you are also aware that my husband is the love of my life. That is not going to change."

"That is the one thing I know and love about you, but I don't want to end our friendship because of what some people think. I guess I will have to find a girlfriend so people will settle down."

She laughed. "You got anybody in mind?"

"Maybe I will find somebody tomorrow."

About that time the meal arrived. "I have been looking forward to this." Nate motioned to the waiter. "Would you bring us another bottle of this wine?"

"You said that we may not be in the same unit when we get back to the front. We have not received any orders yet. What about you?"

"At the end of the week, I am going to a staff meeting. I will know more about what is going on then."

Millie and Willa

Nate and Rosemary were wrong. They were in the same unit, and in February they were very close to the border of Southern Germany. They were moving fast. Everyone knew that the war would soon be over.

By the first week of April, the Germans still had not surrendered. The mobile hospital unit was set up not far from Bavaria and not a great distance from Munich.

For the moment things were quiet.

Working out of a series of tents, the field hospital was busy for about two weeks getting things organized because it looked like they were not going to move again. Nate, Rosemary, and several others were standing around a large oil drum that had been converted into a fire pit one day when they saw a young boy who was about 12 years old walking into the camp. He came up to the group around the fire and in broken English said, "Mother needs a doctor."

The chief officer of the camp came up and said, "Does anybody know what this boy wants?"

Nate spoke up. "I think he said his mother needs a doctor."

The officer wanted to help, but he knew that there were regulations that prevented him from doing so. "Tell him this is an American camp, not a German one and he must leave. Tell him to see if he can find a German doctor."

Nate scoffed. "Good grief, Sir. Where is he going to find a German doctor?"

"I don't know. It is not our problem."

"Well, I care, and it is our problem. I am going with him. If I can help, I am going to."

"No! You are not. You are staying here and that is an order."

"Yes! I am going with him, and when I get back you can court-martial me." He stepped into his tent and got a field kit and a few other supplies.

When he came out of his tent, a few men had pulled a Jeep around, and he motioned for the boy to get in. Rosemary climbed into the back. "I am going too."

"Are you sure you want to do this? There could be some danger, and you heard the colonel. He gave an order not to go. We both could be court marshaled."

"I don't think so. The colonel is not going to risk losing you from his staff, and if I get into trouble, you will save me, or I may get to go home early."

The young boy pointed to the road ahead, and they pulled out of the camp. Speaking in perfect German, Nate said. "Wo ist deine Mutter?"

Rosemary had a surprised look on her face. *How in the heck does he speak German?*

"Ca fünf Kilometer," The young boy replied.

It was not long until they pulled up to a small building off the road. Nate and Rosemary took the medical supplies and went inside. There they found a woman of about thirty on a bed. She was in pain. "Ich sehe, dass Sie ein Kind erwarten. Wann ist es fällig?" Nate asked.

"Jetzt." The woman replied.

Nate turned to Rosemary. "Looks like we are going to have to deliver a baby."

Nate took his stethoscope and listened to the woman's heart and stomach, moving his scope to different areas of her body. "Her heartbeat is good, and so is the baby's. We do have a slight problem."

Nate felt the woman's belly and said to Rosemary in English, "The baby is breech and due now. It is too late to turn the little scrapper."

Nate turned his attention to the woman. "Can you speak any English? I need to give you instructions and my nurse needs to hear them also."

The woman said, "I can speak English."

"Good, what is your name?"

Gritting her teeth, she said, "My name is Willa."

"Listen, Willa. Your baby wants to come into this world feet first. That is not good. I want you to try to relax, and when your contractions come, do not push. When the baby starts to come, we need to be quick."

Turning to Rosemary, he said. "Get me a needle out of the bag and some morphine. We are not going to give her much. We want to relax her but not the baby."

Rosemary quickly opened the field kit and handed a needle to Nate. Giving the shot to the woman he said, "Let's give that a minute to do its magic."

When Nate could see Willa begin to relax a little, he continued to give her an examination. "She is fully dilated. She is ready."

Nate performed his little miracle and a few minutes later, he was holding a little girl. He handed the little bundle to Rosemary and leaned down and kissed Willa on the forehead. "Du hast ein Mädchen," he said in German.

Willa gave Nate a big smile and looked toward Rosemary, who was cleaning up the little girl.

When Rosemary had the baby completely clean, she handed her to Willa. "What are you going to name her?"

She smiled and looked at Nate. "What is your name?"

Nate smiled. He knew what Willa was going to do. "Nate, which is short for Nathan."

"Then we will name her Natalie. We will call her Nata."

"Thank you. That is my sister's name. We must get back to camp. I am leaving a bottle of pills. Take one a day until they are all gone." Nate had not noticed before, but there were two other children in the building besides the young boy. "Where is your husband?"

"He is hiding. He was a soldier, and he knows the war is lost. I fear for what is going to happen to us. If our soldiers find him, he will be shot. I hope the Americans find him first, and I hope all Americans are as kind as you."

Rosemary and Nate stepped outside, and Rosemary said, "There are some supplies in the back of the Jeep. There is a box of rations, a couple of blankets. There is also a box of chocolate bars."

"I guess the colonel will have us charged with stealing also."

"No. He directed the men to put them there. He couldn't let you go, but I am sure he wanted someone to go. I think he knew you well enough to know you would step forward."

They carried the supplies back inside. The three children were all standing around their mother's bed and looking at their new sister. Nate opened the box of chocolate bars and gave one to each child. They just held their candy and looked at Nate. Nate took another candy bar out of the box, opened it, and took a bite. The children slowly unwrapped their bars and reluctantly took a small bite. A big smile came to their faces.

Nate and Rosemary returned to the Jeep. Nate looked over at Rosemary and said, "Aren't you going to ask?"

"No. When you want to tell me, you will."

She paused. "I changed my mind! How in the hell do you speak German?"

"We have crossed the border into Germany. You automatically pick up the language." He then gave a big laugh. "I will explain to you over coffee when we get back to camp."

Dark Times

The night before they were to leave, Millie wrote a letter to her aunt and uncle explaining what she was doing. Early in the morning in late June, Millie met Frank at a small café that opened early and was close to the border. There they sat and drank coffee, and Frank explained what was going to happen. "From this time on, we are not Frank and Millie. My name is Oscar, and you are Anna." He handed her the false documents.

Frank and Millie finished their coffee, left the café, and crossed the border. Once they had cleared the border and moved into the forest, there was a trail that went down a hill. Millie was surprised that Frank seemed to know so much about the area. They had to make their way down a very steep mountain to find the road. Two times they had to hide when they spotted German guards. Once they reached the road, Frank explained that they would have to walk about five miles to the meeting point. It took over an hour to reach the point where the car should have been waiting. No one was there.

"Frank, what should we do? We can't walk to Munich."

"We will wait. If no one comes in an hour we will make our way back to the border. I feel they will be here. They may have had some trouble along the way. We don't need to stay where we can be seen. Let's move into the trees where we can see the road."

In about forty minutes they heard a vehicle coming up the dirt road. They continued to hide in the bushes and waited. It was the two men they were waiting for.

Frank stepped out into the road, and the car stopped and both men got out. "We had just about given up. What happened?"

The taller of the two men spoke first. "You have heard the British and Americans have invaded France. We thought that would distract the police and the army, but just the opposite has occurred. The whole area is alive with the Gestapo."

Frank and the two men walked over to Millie. Frank said, "This is Lars and his brother Abe. They are going to take us the rest of the way." Millie wondered if that was really their names.

The taller of the men, whose name was Lars, turned to Millie. "Do you have your papers? Let me see them." After looking at the papers he said, "These will have to do. If we are stopped, don't talk. Don't say a word unless they ask you a question. Let me do the talking. If they suspect you are not who you say you are, I am going to tell them you are a Jew, and that we are bringing you to them. Do you have the money?"

Millie had a scared look on her face. "You knew upfront that this trip would involve a great deal of risk. If they think you are a Jew, they will arrest you, and you will end up in a prison camp. The war can't go on much longer, and perhaps you will be freed within a year, maybe sooner. If they think you are a spy, they will shoot you on the spot. Do you understand?"

Millie handed Lars the money, and the four of them got into the car and started down the dirt road. They had only gone about twenty kilometers when they came to a German checkpoint.

"Get your papers ready," Lars said as he began to slow the car to a stop. "It is not the Gestapo. We will be okay here."

The German guard was a big man, and he was flanked by two others holding machine guns.

Lars turned to face Frank and Millie in the back seat. "Give me your papers." He got out of the car and said something to the guard.

Millie could clearly hear the conversation. The German guard said, "You came through here earlier, and there were only two of you. Who is with you now?"

"Friends. Oscar and Anna are going to Munich. We have family there, and I understand the Americans have bombed the city. We need to check on our families." He handed the guard the papers.

The guard looked in the back seat and saw Millie and Frank. Looking at Frank he said, "Why are you not in the Army?"

"I am Swiss. This is my cousin. She is German, and we are going to Munich to visit her parents."

The guard handed the papers back to Frank and Millie. "You are going to be stopped several times between here and Munich. Keep these papers handy."

The rail that blocked the road was raised, and the four of them moved on. Millie could feel her heart beating. Once she settled down, she said, "I have not seen any road signs. I wonder how long we will have to stay on this road. We can't be too far from Munich?"

Abe turned around and faced the back seat. "They have taken all the signs down. They fear an invasion, and they hope the signs being gone will cause some confusion. They must think the Americans are stupid. If the Americans cross our borders, they will know more about this country than we do."

They were close to Munich when they came to a second roadblock. This time it was staffed by the Gestapo. Lars said, "We got trouble. Let me do the talking. If we can get through this checkpoint, we are home free."

They pulled up to the checkpoint and stopped. Everyone was shocked when Frank quickly got out of the car and extended his arms in the air. "Take me to Colonel Klein. Do not let this car pass until I have talked to the colonel." Several men surrounded the car and pointed their guns at the two men in the front seat. They did not see Millie in the back.

"What in the hell is going on?" Abe said to Lars.

Lars shifted in his seat and said, "I think we have been had."

In just a few minutes Frank and a Gestapo officer came to the car. "Everyone, out of the car!" the officer shouted. When the three remaining occupants got out of the car, they were ordered to put their hands on top of their heads. "So, you two are the brothers who have been causing us so much trouble. I think we are going to solve that problem very shortly. Give me your papers."

Lars and Abe turned their papers over to the colonel. "Mr. Christian says that you claim to be Swiss. My report says you are working for the underground. Why are you transporting a Jew into Germany? I thought you scum got paid to transport them out."

Millie noticed that the colonel referred to Frank by his real name.

Neither of the two men said anything. The colonel then spoke. "Our information tells us that you work for the underground and take jobs like this to raise money for your misguided cause. It also tells us that you are assassins. Mr. Christian tells us that you got paid to transport Anna or whatever her real name is, to take her to Munich." The colonel got very close to Abe. "Where is the money?"

Abe said nothing. The colonel pulled out his Luger pistol and shot Lars in the leg. "I will not repeat myself a second time. Where is the money?"

Despite the pain, Lars did not fall to the ground. "It is under the front floorboard of the car on the passenger side, under the mat."

Colonel Klein said in a stern voice, "Get the money and bring it to me." He then looked at Millie. "And who are you?"

Frank, who was standing next to the colonel, said, "She is a German Jew. Her name is Millie Becker Berenson. She does not even know the two brothers. She is paying them to get her to Munich."

"Is this so, my dear? Is this your real name?"

Frank came to Millie. "I am sorry, Millie. I didn't want to involve you in this, but I needed a way to trap these two men."

Millie did not say anything. She decided she would not give any information. If the Germans got any information, it would have to come from Frank.

The colonel waited for just a minute and then said, "Mr. Christian says your name is Millie Becker Berenson. Is this true and are you a Jew?"

Millie said nothing.

He smacked Millie across the face. "You will find that I am not a patient man. Before the day ends you will know that Colonel Klein gets what he wants. Take these two men and see if you can get any more information from them."

Colonel Klein turned to Frank and said, "Mr. Christian, you have done well." He handed Frank the envelope which contained the money found under the front floorboard of the car. "Your service is greatly appreciated. There is a reward for these two men. Go to the office and get your money, and then take the car and go back to Switzerland. Contact us if you have any more information."

Frank looked at Millie and said, "You have more money. You will not need it where you are going." After Frank got his money, he got into the car, turned it around, and left. Colonel Klein took Millie to his office and asked her name again. She again said nothing, and the colonel smacked her across the face a second time. "Mr. Christian told me your name. You are a Jew, yes?"

Millie reached up and wiped the blood from the corner of her mouth. She was too scared to talk, and she just stood there.

Colonel Klien walked over and looked out the window. "You know those two men that you hired to transport you are going to be shot. If I do not get some answers from you, you will join them. So, Ms. Berenson, you are a Jew? Do you also work for the underground?"

Millie said nothing. The colonel came back to her and smacked her across the face a third time. "I said do you work for the underground?" Again, Millie said nothing. "Let's look at your papers again."

He picked up the papers from his desk and said, "It says here you are Anna Beck? Do you know the penalty for having false papers? I guess you don't. You are to be shot."

Millie knew there was no reason to not tell the truth, and she looked down at the floor. She remembered what she had been told by Abe and Lars. If they think you are a spy, they will shoot you, but if you are a Jew, they put you in a camp. She struggled to talk. "I am a Jew. My mother and father live in Munich. I have not heard from them for several years. I paid Lars and Abe to take me there. Frank made me the false papers."

The colonel again smacked her across the face. "I know who you are. You are a filthy swine. I think you are also a spy. Jews are trying to get out of Germany. You are paying to get in."

At about that time a loud noise came from outside, and the windows of the office were blown out. Colonel Klein and Millie were blown across the room and fell to the floor. The Colonel was getting up when a young German soldier came running into the office. "colonel, you need to get into a shelter. Two American fighters are attacking us. They are turning and going to make a second pass. Hurry."

The two fighters did make a second pass. When they left, eight Germans had been killed. The colonel was wounded, and when he returned to his office Millie was lying unconscious on the floor. "Pick her up and see if she is still alive." Millie was placed into a chair, and when she regained her senses, she could see the colonel had a severe wound on his left arm.

One of the aides said, "Colonel Klein, we need to get you to a hospital."

The colonel looked at Millie. "In the attack, your two friends have escaped into the forest. We will find them. Meanwhile, we are sending you to Dachau."

She was tied by both her hands and feet and was left lying prone in the back of the truck. The road was rough, and she was tossed around so much she got sick. She tried to close her eyes but that made it worse. When it started to rain, it was both a relief and more anguish. The Germans pulled the truck to the side of the road and left her lying in the back of the truck in the rain.

The next day she was processed into the prison camp. "Where are her papers," the officer in charge of processing prisoners into the camp asked.

"She has no papers," one of the soldiers replied. "Colonel Klein was preparing her when we were attacked yesterday. I am sure they will be sent later."

"Do you even know her name?"

"Yes. Her name is Millie Becker Berenson."

In the next hour, Millie was stripped and given other clothes to wear. Her head was shaven, and she received a number tattooed on her arm. She was in a daze when she was taken back to a stalag. The stalag in which she was placed was crowded with women. She made her way to the back and found a place to lie down. She heard one of the women say, "You are lucky. The woman who had that space died yesterday."

A day later she was assigned to the laundry. They started to work at 7:00 in the morning and worked until 7:00 at night. The work was hard, and they were not given much food. In the morning they were given only a weak coffee and sometimes a weak tea. It was never sweetened. At noon they were given a soup made from potatoes or rutabaga with a small amount of flour in it. They were also given a piece of black bread, and for dinner, they were given only bread. Millie could tell she was losing weight after only two weeks of living in the camp.

Millie lost all track of time. Days turned into weeks and weeks turned into months. The winter months were hard, but they did get some good news. Some of the prisoners overheard the guards saying the Americans were coming from the west and they should abandon the camp. To some, this was good news because they thought they would be freed, but others thought the Germans might kill them all.

In the spring, the work in the camp stopped, and even less food was given to the prisoners. She was aware that there was much activity going on in the camp, but she was barely alive. Only semi-aware of what was going on, she was lying on her mattress. She was cold so she used what strength she had and got under the mattress. She could hear other women saying the Germans had left the camp and Americans were coming through the gate. Millie did not move. She closed her eyes and felt at peace. This is what dying is like she thought.

Prison Camp

The air was crisp and cool with a hint of snow in the air. He heard a commotion and looking toward the main road he saw lots of movement. "What is going on," he asked.

"There is a prison camp north of here. It is full of starving prisoners. Many are going to die if we don't help."

At first, Nate thought it was a prison for P.O.W.'s, but he later found out it was a camp with mostly Jews.

That afternoon, Nate and the medical team worked with the starving men and women who were near death. Many died, and Nate felt like he was going to be sick, but he continued to work. Two days later, he was going through the camp. Many of the camp's prisoners had been moved to tents. He was caught off guard when he heard the sound of someone moaning. He went into the stalag and moved a dirty mattress, and under it, he found a prisoner still alive. The prisoner's head had been shaved, but the hair had started to grow back and looked to be grey. He could not tell if the prisoner was a man or woman. He picked the prisoner up and estimated that the weight of the person was about eighty pounds. He carried the sick person to the camp gate and met two aides who had a stretcher. He called them over and told them to place the sick prisoner on the stretcher and take him or her to the field hospital.

One of the young men said, "We would like to, but we have orders to take this stretcher to Captain Whaley's medical tent."

"Your orders are being changed. Take my patient to the field hospital."

"We are going to get into trouble if we follow your orders."

"You are going to get into more trouble if you don't. The fact that you are taking a stretcher to a medical tent means a patient who is receiving

31

care is being moved. My patient has not received any care. Do as I tell you. You are not going to get into any trouble. I will take one end of the stretcher and the other one of you can find another stretcher."

Once Nate had the patient inside the hospital tent, he discovered that he was working with a woman. She was hollow-eyed, bald, and her skin was grey and full of bedsores and bug bites.

While he was doing his examination, he was joined by Rosemary. "What do you have?"

"I found her in one of the stalags. She had been overlooked. I would give her chances of living about one in a thousand. We need to get her cleaned up. Give her a sponge bath and a clean gown. Be careful with her skin. That is going to be our major problem. I am going to set up an IV, and then we will see if she can take any liquid."

Working with the prisoner, they were able to feed the woman about eight ounces of water. Rosemary took her blood pressure and temperature. "Seventy over forty, and her temperature is low. If we have this much trouble getting water down her there is no chance she can swallow any food."

Nate used his stethoscope to listen to his patient's heart. "Well, that is the only positive thing we have going for us. Her heart is regular but weak. Why don't you get some rest? I am going to stay with her and see if I can get more water down her from time to time."

The next day the camp got the word that the war in Europe was over. A team was going to Munich to try to find a building that would be suitable for a hospital. When Rosemary came into the tent, she relieved Nate, and he took a short nap. When he returned, he found the woman's condition had not changed.

"We have got to get some food into her. She was able to swallow about ten ounces of water last night. I have an idea." Nate got up, went to the motor pool, and checked out a Jeep. He got two soldiers to accompany him and went back to see Willa.

She was still at the house, and she hugged him. "How are things going Willa? I have come to ask a favor, but let me do a quick examination of Nata while I am here."

"We got the food you sent, and I don't know how we could ever repay you for your kindness."

Nate walked over to the crib where Nata was asleep. "Well, there is a way. I said I needed a favor. If you don't want to do what I am going to request I will understand, and we will still be friends."

Willa had some concerns, but she did not show them. "What is it?"

"I have a patient back at the field hospital who has been starved to the point of death. She cannot eat, and even if she could I am afraid she could not keep it down. I want some mother's milk to see if she can swallow it and keep it down. If she can do this, I would need enough to feed her for about a week, and would need enough for about two times a day."

"She is Jewish, isn't she?"

Nate looked down at the floor. "Does it matter?"

"No. Of course not. You have shown me that people are people. How do we do this?"

"I have a pump."

When Nate left the house, he noticed three children standing by his Jeep. He smiled at them. "I know what you want." He reached in the back of the Jeep and pulled out a bag that had six chocolate bars. "Eat one now and save the others for a snack later."

When Nate returned to the hospital, Rosemary was not with the patient, but another nurse was sitting with her. "Rosemary was called to headquarters. Something has come up. Something good, I think."

"You are Carolyn. We have not worked together very much. I need a baby bottle. Is there any way you could find one?"

"I think I can help you with that," and she got up and left.

About thirty minutes later, Carolyn returned with a bottle.

They had about everything ready when Rosemary returned. "I see things are ready to go. I pray that nature will do its thing and she will take to the bottle."

Nate took the bottle, wet the nipple, and pushed it gently into her mouth. They waited and nothing happened. They continued to wait and then the weakened woman's involuntary muscles started to work, and she started taking the milk. She continued like a hungry baby until all the mother's milk was gone.

Nate put his arms around the two nurses and hugged them. "That is half the battle. It has got to stay down."

Three hours later they gave the patient a bottle a second time, but this time with warm water and again they were successful. She took the third bottle of baby's milk that night and had had four bottles of water that day.

The next day Nate secured enough baby's milk for a second day, and Willa was delighted that her milk was helping save a life. After they had fed the patient, Nate and Rosemary went to the mess tent and had breakfast and coffee. "Was your news good or bad yesterday?"

"It was good. I do not know how to tell you any other way, but just to blurt it out. I am going home. I am being released in a few days. I can't wait to see Jim. But I am sad. I have never had a better friend than you. We must keep in contact."

"I couldn't be happier for you. But you are right. I have had only two good friends in my life, you and my sister. We will stay in touch. Do you know when you are leaving?"

"They are going to let me know. I would say in the next couple of weeks, maybe sooner. I think it will be determined by when transportation is available."

The next day Nate went back to Dachau and was able to find a list of the prisoners and their numbers. *One thing about the Germans, they keep good records, h*e said to himself. Looking down the list he found the number, 90718. Millie Becker Berenson. There was no other information other than when she came into the camp. *My goodness, she was here almost a year.* When he returned to the hospital, he put her name on the record sheet and started talking to her, calling her Millie.

The medical team was able to find a building inside Munich that had once been a school and had minor damage. A team of engineers was able the get the building ship shape in just a few days. Nate moved most of his patients, including Millie, to the new hospital.

Changes in Millie's health were slight. After a week, Nate changed the formula to whole milk and the results were the same. Two days later she could swallow some soft food, but her skin was making no improvement.

Nate got a message. *"Come to headquarters, urgent." What have I done now*, he thought? His first thoughts were that doctoring Millie was a problem. When he arrived, he was taken right in and greeted by Colonel Lawson. "Take a seat, Doctor Weber."

"What is this all about?"

"Relax, there is no trouble here. Do you know the name Logan Taylor?"

Nate looked at the colonel. "I have heard that name. He is a senator or something."

"Yes, and that 'or something' is that he is here in Munich. He is here for two reasons. He is on a powerful committee making decisions about what is going to happen here after the war. The second 'or something' is why you are here. He has a son. His son is Captain Logan Taylor Jr. He was shot just before the surrender. He was shot in the back, and the bullet is lodged against his spine. There is some damage to the spine, and doctors have been scared to take the bullet out. Worst case scenario is that removing the bullet will kill him, and the best-case scenario is he will be paralyzed. He is being flown here by chopper and will be here in the morning. He has been in a field hospital near Nuremberg that is being closed. Doctors who have been working with him think that he may not even survive the trip here. Senator Taylor asked for the best surgeon on my staff, and that is why you are here. I have his x-rays and records here. Study them tonight and have your team ready tomorrow. I have heard you have magic in the operating room. If you do, you are going to need it. Do your best." He handed a large envelope to Nate. "Let us hope that when you go into his wound it is not as bad as the x-rays show."

That night, Nate opened the large envelope that contained Logan Taylor's medical records and other information from the doctors who had worked on his back wound. He first looked at the x-rays. *Good grief. That bullet should have gone completely through his back. He should be dead.* He then started to read the medical notes. He found that Captain Taylor Jr. had been shot by a sniper using a Mauser K98 rifle. His men had found the sniper and killed him. The bullet had first gone through a backpack and Logan's supply belt before it entered his back. *This slowed the projectile down. Therefore, he is still alive.*

The next morning Rosemary, Nate, and three other doctors were in the ready room. Nate had hung five x-rays up against a light board for all to see.

"We are going to operate on Captain Taylor once we have become familiar with his condition. It is not a routine operation. I have looked at his records and re-looked at them. There is a one in five chance he is not going to survive. He has been shot in the back with the bullet lodged against his spine. If we remove the bullet, he may not live. Our only hope is the x-rays are not showing us everything. There are several fragments from the bullet, and it looks like there are also some bone fragments we will have to deal with. If he lives, there is a good chance he will be paralyzed. Here is the kicker. His father is here. He is Senator Logan Taylor. Just the operation is pressure enough. If things go south, I am responsible. We will do the best we can, and if that is not enough, then so be it. You need to study the x-rays and be ready for the operation when I get back. I am going to see this captain and see what his attitude is about this operation. I want him positive. That is important for him to get through this and accept the outcome, good or bad. One other thing. He is an extremely sick man. In my opinion, he is not going to live very long if we don't operate and get that bullet out."

About that time, Carolyn came into the room. "Captain Taylor is prepped, and we can start when the team is ready."

Logan Taylor Jr.

When Nate came into the operating room, Captain Taylor was face down on the operating table. Nate walked up to him and said, "Are you ready? Today is your day."

Captain Taylor was sarcastic. "You are very cheerful. You do not have to be. Before I got here, other doctors were very frank about my situation. There can be no good outcome for me from this. I know that my legs are paralyzed. You are not going to fix that. The best outcome is for me to die."

Nate stayed cheerful. "Your father is here. Has he been to see you?"

"He has, and I refused to see him."

"What good did that do? He is going to worry about you just the same, and all you are doing is adding to his grief. Rethink your decision about seeing him. You said that you had been briefed about your condition. I must be honest. There is a chance that you might not live through this operation. Do not do this to your father. See your father. Seeing someone who loves you will help you too. Do you have somebody waiting for you back home?"

"I did. I was engaged to be married. I wrote and called it off. I didn't want her waiting for someone who might not return or if he did might be paralyzed."

"That was noble and stupid. Even though they cannot hear me I sometimes like to talk to my patients during the operation. Shall I call you Logan or Captain?" Nate was just making conversation to break through to the captain. He never talked to his patients during operations.

"I was named for my father. I hate being called Logan Taylor Jr. As soon as people hear my name they start asking about my father and I lose all identity. I prefer my middle name, which is Ray. Call me Ray. Just plain Ray."

"What is the name of this young lady?"

"Her name is Sydney Ann Mitchell. I call her Sam."

"How do you get Sam out of Sydney?"

For the first time, Ray smiled. "You are not very smart, are you doctor? It is her initials."

"Smart enough not to make decisions about the outcome of an operation until I have all the facts. We must see your wound up close. We are not going to open the original wound. We are going to open an area just to the right of the bullet. Clean up what is there and then have a good look at the bullet. In your records, it says you cannot feel your legs. We will see what is causing that. Who knows, we just might be able to fix you. There are a couple of things I do know. If you think you are going to die, you just might, and if you think you are going to live, you just might. I tell you what. In the next couple of days, you and I are going to write Sam a letter and tell the young lady to tear the first letter up. She is a young lady? You are not marrying an old woman, are you?"

For the second time, Ray smiled.

"I am going to send your father in here. Tell him you are going to make it even if you don't believe it. Make him feel better."

After Ray's father left the room, Nate came back in. "Rosemary is going to give you a shot. It will not put you to sleep, but it will relax you." Ray closed his eyes and started thinking about the past few years.

Logan Ray Taylor had lived a charmed life. He grew up in New York City with his mother and father. He had one sister who was two years younger than himself. His father was in politics and was a friend of Franklin Roosevelt. When Roosevelt was elected president in 1932, he appointed Logan Taylor Sr. to an advisory committee. In 1938, his father was sent to Germany as a special envoy to try to keep some control of the rising tensions between the United States and Germany.

In the spring of 1941, two things happened to Ray Taylor. He graduated from military school, and he met Sydney Ann Mitchell. Sydney was from an upper-middle-class family.

Ray was sitting in a small outdoor restaurant close to Times Square. He had not ordered his food when Sydney walked up to his table.

"Hey, General. I like your uniform."

Ray looked up and saw one of the most beautiful girls he had ever seen. "I can only assume you must be crazy."

She gave him a strange look. "Why would you say that?"

"Here you are the most beautiful girl I have ever seen and could have any man you wanted for a boyfriend, and here you are flirting with me."

"I am not flirting with you. They say that a war may be coming soon. I wanted to find a way to talk with you and let you know how I respect the men who may be protecting this nation. Perhaps I did it badly. I am sorry."

"I am sorry too. Please forgive me and have a seat. My name is Ray. I am just going into military service. What might your name be?"

"My name is Sydney, but everyone calls me Sam."

He stood up and pulled out a chair. "Nice to meet you, Sam. I am curious. How do you get Sam from Sydney?"

"It is quite simple. My full name is Sydney Ann Mitchell."

As they sat and talked, he found out that she was a student at New York University, and that she had been on several dates but did not have a steady boyfriend. She liked sports, reading, and going to the movies. He told her that he lived in New York, but he was going to Fort Meade. They left the restaurant and continued to talk as they walked into the park.

"What are you doing the rest of the day?"

"I don't know, what do you have in mind?

Ray stopped walking and turned and faced Sam. "This is going to sound crazy. I have promised my dad that I would have dinner with him and my sister tonight. I want you to join us."

"Man, you sure do move fast. We just met and you are already asking me to meet your family. I noticed you didn't mention your mother. Are your parents separated?"

"My mother passed away several years ago. The truth is that I do not get to see my father very much, and I want to go to dinner with him, but this has been one of the nicest days I have had in a long time, and I don't want the day to end. My dad can be a little stiff, but you will love my sister. I think that you two will forget that Dad and I are even at the table."

"I may be a little crazy too. Where is this little shindig going to be?"

"McAllister's."

"Good grief, I can't go to McAllister's dressed like this. I need to go home and dress up."

A big smile spread across Ray's face. "That means you will join us?"

"I understand that McAllister's has a waiting list and that you must make reservations days or months in advance. How can I just join you?"

"Don't worry. Dad has a way of getting things done. If I were bringing my whole outfit, I am sure he could get all of us in. You will need to give me your address and I will pick you up."

"What time is the reservation? I will meet you there."

When Sam arrived at McAllister's she realized she did not know the name on the reservation. Ray had not told her his last name. She saw the maitre d and said, "This is silly. I am to meet my party here, and I don't know the name on the reservation."

The maître d smiled, "Are you, Sam?"

"Yes, I am."

"Please follow me."

Sam had never been to McAllister's. She was surprised at how big it was but was not surprised at its elegance. When they approached the table, she saw Ray and his father. His father looked familiar.

"Sam, this is my father, Logan Taylor. Dad, this is Miss Sydney Ann Mitchell."

"Nice to meet you, Miss Mitchell."

Mr. Taylor got up and pulled out a chair. Sam thought to herself, *I have seen photos of Mr. Taylor in the newspaper. He is famous.* Sam was not sure what she should say. "I see there are only three of us. I hope I am not taking the place of your daughter."

Logan Taylor gave a half-smile. "No, not at all. Leslie is always late. She will be here at any moment."

Ray was right. The conversation was stiff for about ten minutes. Then Leslie came bouncing to the table and everything changed. "Junior, you look different. I believe you have picked up some weight. Looks good on you. Who is the chick?"

Sam could not help but smile. She started to introduce herself, but Ray spoke first. "This is my friend Sam. We met in Times Square today. We became instant friends."

Sam was embarrassed. "It does look a little strange. Here Ray and I just met a few hours ago, and here I am eating with his family."

Logan Taylor Sr. said, "Not strange at all. Some people you meet become instant friends and some people you have known for a lifetime are always strangers."

This made Sam feel better, and she relaxed. She turned and faced Leslie. "You called Ray 'Junior'. Where does that come from?"

Logan Sr. chuckled. "Junior does not like his name."

Ray gave his father a frown. "Dad, you know that is not true." He turned and faced Sam. "Dad is somewhat famous. When I meet new people and they hear my name, the first thing out of their mouth is, are you related to Logan Taylor the…. By the way Dad, what title have you now?"

"Special envoy to England. In about a week, I will be in England."

Leslie was shocked. "You are going to a war zone."

"I will be safe. I will be leaving at the end of the week."

Logan Taylor Sr. quickly changed the subject. He started asking questions about Sam and her family and her future. When the meal was over, two separate conversations developed. Ray was talking with his father and Leslie and Sam to each other. Senator Taylor was right. Leslie and Sam were instant friends.

Ray stood up from the table. "I am going to take Sam home, and I will see you two a little later on."

Sam got up from the table. "You don't have to take me home. I think I can find my way."

"What do you mean, you can find your way? Are you going to walk?"

Sam gave a quick smile. "No. I am taking a taxi. Thank you, Mr. Taylor, for a wonderful evening. Be safe in England."

Ray took Sam by the arm and escorted her to the door. "I am going to see you to your door and take the taxi back to my home."

"Ray, you don't have to do that."

"Yes, I do. I want to make this day last as long as I can."

Sam was pleased because she felt the same way.

Standing in front of her door, Ray said, "So this is where you live. It is very nice."

"Well, yes and no. I have a dorm room on campus." Sam was blushing a little when she said, "Do you want to meet again tomorrow?"

"Yes, yes I do. When and where?"

Sam and Ray met every day till he had to report back to Fort Meade. He wrote her once a week and called her as often as he could. Sometimes he would get a three-day pass, and when he did, he would head for New York. Ray did not get an extended leave until Thanksgiving. By then, Ray and Sam were in love. He spent Thanksgiving Day with Sam's family. That same day Ray asked Sam to marry him, and she said yes. Sam wanted a big wedding, so they set a date for the summer of 1942. Ray had about three days left in his leave when the Japanese bombed Pearl Harbor. Sam wanted to get married right away, but Ray did not. He convinced her the war would be short because he felt the Pacific Ocean was too large and the United States would soon make a peace with the Japanese. Ray left Sam on December 10 and reported back to Fort Meade. Ray had told Sam that he would most likely be sent to San Diego and then stationed somewhere in the Pacific. His thinking all changed when Germany declared war on the United States on December 11.

Early in 1942, Ray found himself in England and was in the 7th Army. In November, his unit took part in Operation Torch. It was his first combat but would not be his last. After Torch, he was promoted to captain. His unit was part of the invasion of Sicily and later fought near Rome. After the invasion of France, he was moving across Southern France and as the Germans were pushed back, he found himself in the Rhineland.

In April of 1945, Ray's unit was fighting near Nuremberg. It was some of the most intense fighting of the war. Near the end of a firefight, his unit had the upper hand. Ray was lying on his stomach and looking at a map. The fighting had stopped. He took off his backpack and put it next to his side. That was the last thing he remembered.

Nate had told Ray that the shot would only relax him, but he had not gotten a lot of sleep and had gone into a deep sleep. The team was standing looking at the x-rays and charts when Nate entered the operating room.

Doctor Edwards pointed at one of the x-rays. "There are some bone fragments around the bullet. Are we going to remove the bullet and then come back later to remove the fragments?"

Nate pointed to an x-ray. "We are going to remove the fragments first. Some are bone, and some are fragments from the bullet. While we are doing that, I hope we can get a view of the bullet and maybe we can assess how to best proceed."

Doctor Black said, "He might not have any feeling in his legs and no movement because of the bullet or swelling. The nerves could still be intact. You are going to have to have a very steady hand if you can get near the bullet. We can't just go in there and yank it out."

"We are going to have to be slow and steady. We will move the bullet millimeters at a time until we can assess how much nerve damage is done." Nate looked at the three nurses on the team. "You nurses are going to have to wipe a lot of sweat off the foreheads of us doctors today."

"Rosie, I need you to monitor his blood pressure. Carolyn, you will be assigned to me. Doctor Edwards will assist me, and everybody else knows what to do."

Rosemary said, "I have four pints of whole blood ready to go."

Nate said to his team, "Get him ready. I am going to check on Millie, and I will be here about the time you have him ready."

Nate walked to the room where Millie was. He was surprised. Willa was sitting with her and was holding her hand. "How is she doing?"

Nate gave Willa a quick smile. "The same. No change in blood pressure or temperature and her heart rate is still stable. She is taking some soft food and water. I am glad you came. She needs someone who cares about her."

"Is she getting better? She looks so fragile."

Nate looked at Willa. "She is stable, but she needs more than we can give her. You have kept this lady alive, and on her behalf, I thank you."

"I can't believe that my country did this to her and thousands more. I can't stay. I can't thank you enough for what you have done for me and my family." She then hugged Nate.

"Willa, I want you to do me a favor. Don't ever thank me again."

As Willa left the room, Nate sat down next to Millie and said, "Well Millie, it's time you started getting better. If I mess up today, it might be the end of us both. I must get you to a regular hospital that is equipped to doctor extreme trauma. I need my sister. You need my sister! I need her advice and support, and you need her medical expertise."

As Nate returned to the operating room, he looked at each x-ray. He saw that Ray was now awake.

Doctor Edwards said, "Let us not take too long. I got a date tonight." He looked at Ray and gave him a wink.

Rosemary gave a half-laugh. "Doctor Edwards, You have not had a date since you got here, but everyone knows you have tried."

The young man gave a smile. Nate looked at his team. "Take him under."

Getting to the bullet was slow, and the team was extremely careful with every cut. It took two hours just to have the wound open enough to see the bullet and to remove the bone fragments. It took two more hours until the area was free of fragments and bleeding was controlled enough to get a clear view of the bullet.

Using a magnifier, Doctor Edwards looked at the bullet, which was firmly lodged against a vertebra. "It has broken off part of the spinous process and lodged against the facet, and I can't tell if it has penetrated the foramen."

"Rosie, I need to see the second x-ray." A second nurse helped Nate to take off his gloves and put on a second pair. He looked very carefully at the x-ray. "This x-ray does not help. Hold your breath. I am going to move the bullet a few millimeters and hope this gives us a better view." Nate slowly moved the bullet. "There, everyone relax, and we will wait ten minutes and move it some more."

Doctor Edward looked through the magnifier. "We got some bleeding. It's not much but enough to worry about."

"Rosie, get me a small sponge and let me see if I can clean this up just a little."

Rosie handed the sponge to Nate and watched as he carefully removed the blood from around the bullet. "What are you going to do next?"

"Please wipe my forehead. We need to shock his legs to see if there is any movement."

Rosie moved the electric probes into place. "How much power do you want to start with?"

As Doctor Edwards moved to observe the legs, Nate said, "Twenty-five percent."

As the legs were shocked, Doctor Edwards said, "Nothing."

"Rosie, go to fifty percent."

Rosemary gave another shock to the legs.

"We have some response. It is not much. That bullet must be pressing against some nerves. We will have to get that lead out of there."

Nate made the second move and waited, then the third move and a fourth move and soon the bullet was free of the spine.

"Doctor Edwards, look and tell me what you see." Doctor Edwards moved the magnifier into place. "Looks good. I believe everything is where it should be. I can see the nerves coming out of the column and they look healthy. Wait, we have a problem. There are several small bone fragments between the bullet and the nerves. The nerves look okay. Being this long since he was wounded, they would be shriveled up if they were dead. Nate you are going to have to have a very steady hand to get the fragments out, but we can't let them stay there."

Nate and Doctor Edwards exchanged places. "I am going to use the magnifier to see if I can get to the bone fragments."

The operation took twelve hours. And when they came out of the operating tent, Senator Taylor was waiting.

"Things went well. Much better than expected. We will have to take a wait and see for the next forty-eight hours, but a complete recovery is expected. It could take several weeks or months for the feeling to return to his legs. We can start therapy in about a week."

The senator was delighted. "When will we be able to move him?"

"We would think in about a week, maybe ten days. He should recover quickly."

The ten days passed quickly, but Nate was worried about Millie. She was not stable, and her numbers would go up and down. Her weight had increased some. When she was brought to the hospital, she was sixty-eight pounds, and now she was seventy-two pounds. Still, he worried. He could not tell how old she was, but he guessed she must be between forty-five or fifty. Her hair had grown about a quarter inch and was gray. Senator Taylor was still in Munich, and Nate decided he would ask for a favor.

He was able to get an appointment, and sitting in front of the senator, he received praise and thanks over and over.

"Senator Taylor. I need a favor, and it is not a small one."

"If I can do anything I will. What is it?"

"I have a patient. Her name is Millie Becker Berenson. She was in Dachau. I don't know much about her. She is very ill. Her current weight is only seventy-two pounds. I need to get her to the United States. I need to get her to my sister in Boston. She is a doctor, and she has the skills to save Ms. Berenson's life, and they have the proper facilities to treat her. She is extremely weak and covered with bedsores. She might not even make the trip. Is there anything you can do?"

"Is she a German citizen?"

"I would assume so. I don't have much information about her. The records at the camp were incomplete. I only have a name, but I want to save her. If we can't get her to the United States, is there a way to get her to a hospital in England? Is there anything you can do?"

"No, there is not much. There is hardly any way to get a German immigrant into the US. The quota is near zero. It would be even harder to get a German citizen into England. The paperwork in either case would be extremely slow. But by the time we got the proper paperwork done, she would be either dead or an old woman. I do know that President Truman may release the restrictions on immigration that would help the Jewish people. If he does, he will give displaced children priority. I don't think we can get an adult into the United States for at least a year, and the fact that she is sick makes it impossible. I wish I could help. I have influence, but not that much."

The senator sat back in his chair. He thought for a minute. "There might be a way, but it is extreme. If she were married to a G.I. I could use the War Brides Act. I could get her on my plane to London and another plane to Boston. Yes, it might work. Jr. and I are leaving in four days. You will need to marry her. Are you willing to do that?"

"I will do anything necessary to save her life."

During the next couple of days, the senator pushed every regulation to the limit. Nate took all the steps to marry Millie. Before the marriage, he was called back to the senator's office. "Everything is in place. Once the wedding has taken place, she can leave with me. I need you to know what you are committing to with this wedding. There is a whole lot more than you might have expected." The senator took his time and explained to Nate what he was committing to. When he finished, he looked at Nate and said, "Are you willing to agree to what I have explained to you?"

Nate stood up and extended his hand to the senator. "Yes. I thank you so much for making this happen. She will be ready to leave when you are ready to go."

"As soon as you give the okay for Jr. to travel, I will be ready to go. Are you sending a nurse with her?"

"Yes. Her name is Rosemary Harris. She is leaving the Army and going back to the United States. I have not told her yet, but she and Ms. Berenson will be with you on the flight to England, and from there she will go to Boston."

"How do you know she will want to take on this flight and responsibility?"

"I know Rosemary. She is waiting for transportation to get home, and she is a very good person."

Senator Taylor thought for a minute. "Doctor Weber. I do not want to give you any more to worry about, but I need to bring this up. What if Miss Berenson is a Mrs. Berenson? You know she could have a husband."

"The odds are against it. There was another Berenson listed in the records of the camp, but he was listed as single, and he was too young. If she had a husband, I am sure he would be deceased."

"One more thing. What we are doing is illegal. It is illegal to marry a non-citizen to get them into the United States. There are several documents for me to sign. My name is on them and so is yours. I am going to lose the records of your marriage with a lot of legal red tape. You must stay married for five years. We will hide these documents here in Germany. No one can know our involvement in the United States. That brings us to Millie. We have to keep her in the dark for as long as possible. If she gets better, she is going to want to know who her husband is. Her curiosity can get us all in trouble. Time is our friend."

The next day Nate took the steps to marry Millie. Nate took her hand and signed the documents. Rosemary and Doctor Edwards were going to be witnesses to the wedding. Before the wedding, Nate took Rosemary and Doctor Edwards aside and explained what they were committing to. He explained they could say nothing about how this was done. Rosemary and Doctor Edwards signed as witnesses. Millie had no idea that when she woke up she would be a married woman.

Nate took Rosemary by the hand and said, "Are you ready to get out of here? Have you heard anything about your ride?"

"No. I am playing the waiting game."

"How would you like to leave tomorrow?"

Rosemary looked surprised. "How is that possible?"

"If you wait for transportation, you might be another week or maybe even more. Once you get to London maybe another week. You would then be put on a ship and that would take another seven days. I can have you home in about three or four days, maybe even less."

"What is the catch?"

"Not a big one. You would have to agree to be a nurse for three or four days. That is what you do anyway. Senator Taylor has a plane leaving tomorrow. Millie is going to be on it and going to my sister in Boston. You would have to take care of Senator Taylor's son on the way to London, and Millie to Boston. When you get to London, Senator Taylor will then put you and Millie on a plane to Boston. My sister will meet you at the Boston airport and arrange transportation to your home in Maine."

"I am packed and ready to go. Just tell me where to meet the senator."

"An ambulance will pick you, Millie, and Ray up in the morning to take you to the airfield north of Munich. Then you will be off."

He looked at his watch. "I need to call Natalie. It is up in the morning in Boston. I will see you off tomorrow."

Nate was able to catch his sister at the hospital. She was more than excited to hear from him. "Look, Natalie, I don't have much time, and I need a favor. I have written to you about my patient Millie. I am sending her to you. She needs care and lots of it. I will pay for any cost she has. She will be there in about three days. Once her nurse is in London, she will call you and let you know when they will be in Boston."

"Of course. I will do what is necessary to get her back to health. Just how did you pull this off?"

"It is complicated. I will explain in just a moment. I have money in Southwest Bank. You have the power to write checks on it, and you will remember I gave you some checks before I left in case something happened to me. Millie will be accompanied by a nurse named Rosemary Harris. Write a check and cash it, and give Rosemary five thousand dollars."

"You are paying this nurse five thousand dollars to bring Millie to the United States."

"No. She is doing it for free, and just the ride home. I am giving her the money because she and her husband need it, and she has been my best friend during the war. Her husband was wounded, and I am sure they need money to get settled and back on their feet. Now I am going to tell you how I pulled this off. The only way I could get Millie to the United States is to marry her. In the future, I will fix the marriage with an annulment or divorce. Millie at this point does not even know she is married. You will need to tell her when she is back on her feet, but leave me out of the story. I am going to write to you and give you all the details, but you can never discuss this with anybody. The less anyone knows about this marriage, the better. I know nothing about Millie, other than that I want to save her. I think she is a lot older than me, so take care of my old bride." He then gave a big laugh.

Natalie did not say anything for a moment, then said, "Nate, good grief."

United States

Millie had no awareness of the trip from Germany to the United States, or how difficult it had been. When the plane touched down in Boston, Rosemary sighed with relief. Natalie was waiting, and an ambulance was on the tarmac. When Natalie boarded the plane, she was greeted by Rosemary.

"How did it go?"

"Not well. Her blood pressure is down, she has a fever, and she has been non-responsive for the last two hours."

Natalie quickly went to Millie and listened to her heart, and using her hand confirmed she had a fever. Natalie turned to the two paramedics who had boarded the plane with her. "She does feel warm. Load her into the ambulance as quickly as possible. I will ride with her." She then turned to Rosemary. "I have arranged a room for you at a local motel. I also have a bus ticket for you. The ticket is for tomorrow and will get you home in about half a day."

"If you don't mind, I want to go to the hospital with Millie. I want to help make sure she is stable before I leave."

Natalie agreed, and in less than an hour, they had checked Millie into a private room and taken the necessary precautions to make her stable. Two hours later, Millie's temperature was close to normal, and her blood pressure was still low but okay.

"I feel better. I can use that motel now."

"You have done an excellent job getting her here. The way Nate described her condition, I didn't think she would last the flight. Let us go to the cafeteria and get something to eat, and then we will see about getting you to your motel."

The two women picked up their meals and took a seat in a booth. Natalie was about to say something when a tall man came to the booth. "I am sorry I didn't get here sooner, but traffic was murder."

Laying her hamburger down on her plate, Natalie spoke, "Rosemary, this is my husband, Tom. When we finish eating, he will drive you to the motel, and he will also pick you up tomorrow to take you to the bus station."

"Tom, this is Rosemary Harris. She accompanied the patient from Germany."

"Nice to meet you, Tom. Nate said you were a lawyer."

"Yes. Yes, I am. How is old Nate?"

"Busy. When you are good at what you do, you are in demand. I fear he is trying to do too much. He has done a lot to help the prisoners of Dachau make a healthy transition out of the camp. He has tried to save as many as possible. He is also working with the local people to help rebuild relations with the United States. The Jewish people have no place to go. Some are still living at the camp. Something must be done. I don't think Nate will consider leaving until things are improved."

Natalie gave a sarcastic laugh. "You said he has done a lot for the prisoners. Hell, he even married one."

Rosemary only smiled. "You don't know the half of it. I had forgotten how good a good hamburger tastes. Thank you so much."

Just as they finished their meal, an orderly came to the table. "I was told I would find you down here. Your patient is resting comfortably, and blood pressure and temperature are in a safe range. We feel it will be okay for you to go home."

"Thank you. It has been a long day. If she changes during the night call me."

After the young man left the table Natalie reached into her purse and pulled out a thick envelope. "I talked with Nate yesterday and he wanted me to give you this."

Rosemary took the envelope, opened it, and scanned the fifty, one-hundred-dollar bills inside. "I can't take this. Our deal was for me to get home. I am getting home at least three weeks earlier than before. No! I won't take it."

As she handed Natalie the envelope, Natalie pushed it back at her. "He wanted you to have the money. He said that you and your husband might need it to get started. I assure you he can afford the money. I bet you didn't know he was a millionaire. Mom and Dad left us well off. I have one more surprise for you. Your husband is at the hotel waiting for you. He wanted to meet you at the airport, but he knew you would want to come to the hospital, and he was nursing a sore leg. Here are your two bus tickets for tomorrow. If you would like, you can stay a couple of days in Boston. The tickets can be exchanged for a later day."

Lying in bed, Millie was semi-aware of her surroundings. She had no memory of the trip to Boston, which had taken three days. She was unaware that she had been in the Boston hospital for twelve hours, and it was morning the next day. She was aware of the talking of the nurses as they went about their morning routines. *They are not speaking German. Where am I?* She was suddenly aware that her bed was being cranked up, putting her into a sitting position. She strained to open her eyes, but all she could see was light and color and could make out that there was some movement within the colors of light. She could not see, so she closed her eyes and just listened to the nurses going about the room.

Then she felt a hand go around the back of her neck, and she was being pulled forward. "Let me get that pillow and give you a nice fresh one," she heard a kind voice say.

She did not say anything about not being able to see. She said nothing. She just lay there and listened to the people in the room. These were not the same voices she had heard before. She knew what they were saying. She learned English as a child while going to school, took English classes in high school, and had three years of English in college. She spoke English with only a slight accent. All she could figure out was she was in a different bed and a different place than before.

"Time to get some food in you. The doctor will be here at about nine. If you do not eat, she will fuss at me. I have some cream of wheat."

She could feel the spoon touch her lips, and she opened her mouth and was able to swallow the sweet food. It tasted good. She was hungry, and that was a sensation she had not experienced for a while.

"That is the last of it. You did well. Let us see if we can get some of this apple juice in you."

Apple juice. I have not had apple juice for a long while.

In the next hour, she was given a sponge bath. This was a delicate process because of the skin damage from bedsores and bug bites. The food and the bath helped her to relax. She began to have some memories of the last several days, but could not put them all together. She was confused. From the time she had put herself under the mattress until now was filled with just pieces of information. She continued to lie very still and listen to her new world and hope that things would begin to make sense.

After a while, she was left alone, and she drifted back to sleep. When Doctor Elliston came into her room, she picked up her chart and said to herself, "Good, good, good," as she looked at the morning entries. She said something to the nurse that Millie could not make out, and then she started talking to Millie, even though her eyes were closed and looked as if she were still asleep. Millie was not asleep. She was listening to every word.

"Well, your color is good, blood pressure okay, the temperature is normal. I feel good about that." She turned to the nurse. "Were you able to weigh her?"

"Best we could. Looks like her weight is about seventy-two pounds. She ate all her food and drank the juice, but she has made no response to anything spoken to her."

"How did she react to the bath this morning? Did she seem to have discomfort or react to pain?"

"No. She didn't respond at all. She didn't feel any pain when we touched her skin."

"That's not good. Remove her gown. I want to examine her entire body and look closely at each wound. I need more light and a magnifier." Doctor Elliston took her time and looked at Millie's skin. "Many of the areas look like Stage 2 skin damage. The problem is that she didn't seem to feel any pain. Most of the sores are open and many look like scrapes or blisters. She should have felt some pain. I think we can classify most of this as Stage 3. There is going to be damage below the skin's surface. What we have to be concerned about is Stage 4 damage."

"What are you going to do?"

"We need to see if an operating room is available. If it is, get it ready and take her there. I will need a small team. I am going to remove some infected and dead tissue. When she returns to the room she is going to look like a mummy. I am going to wrap her with medicated gauze and a few other special ointments that I have found to be successful in these cases. Doctor Weber did a good job. I think she would have died in less than a week from these skin infections if she had stayed in Germany."

I am not in Germany anymore. Where am I?

After a week of treatments, Millie's skin was losing its grey color, and the wounds were showing they were healing.

As Doctor Elliston came into Millie's room for her daily examination, Nurse Tutor was working with Millie. The nurse had propped her up and was singing.

Natalie smiled and said, "Do you think singing is helping our patient? How are things going?"

"Not good. I was hoping singing would help her some. When I cleaned her this morning she reacted to the pain. You could tell it hurt for her to be touched."

Doctor Elliston took her stethoscope and came to Millie and listened to her heart. Millie reacted to each time she moved the scope to different areas. "This is good. Her heart is strong. She is feeling pain from the wounds, which means the nerve endings are not damaged. Has she opened her eyes?"

"No. She has not. Is she in a coma?"

"I don't think so. Keep singing and talking to her. Things are looking much better. If she is in a lot of pain give her morphine."

For the next three days, Millie was in a state of semi-consciousness. She did not seem to be able to move or open her eyes but was aware of when the nurses were talking to her.

On the fourth day, she was more aware of her surroundings. She could move her arms and was aware of her legs, but they didn't seem to want to move. She opened her eyes hoping she could now see, but the results were still the same. Nothing but light and color. She said nothing but just waited and hoped her vision would come back.

Doctor Elliston and Nurse Tutor were in the room discussing Millie's treatment when Nurse Tutor saw that Millie's eyes were open. "Doctor Elliston, look! She has opened her eyes."

Doctor Elliston reached into her pocket, pulled out a small flashlight, and shone the light into her eyes. She squinted and turned away. "She is aware of us, and she can hear us, but she will not understand what we are saying unless she speaks English."

Speaking in German Doctor Elliston said, "Millie, I know you are scared and don't know where you are. Everything will be explained. Try not to talk just yet."

During the week, food intake was increased, and by the end of the week, Millie was getting more aware of her surroundings. She was scared. She could not see, the only language spoken around her was English, and she had no idea where she was or how she got there. She could not see the nurses, but she could understand them and knew that she was in a hospital.

She had listened to the nurses and knew she had been extremely ill but was getting better. She was no longer feeling the pain from her skin, and she was no longer covered with gauze. She began to enjoy hearing the nurses talk about their families and could identify each one by the sound of their voices.

Millie had been in the hospital for three weeks. She had been raised to a sitting position, and she was aware if there were movements in the room because there were changes in the light and colors she could see.

She was sitting up in her bed and could tell someone had come into the room. She heard the voice that she recognized as the doctor. "I am going to shine a light in your eyes. Try not to squint and try to keep your eyes open and be still."

Millie decided now was the time to try to communicate with the doctor. Speaking in German and a weak, hoarse voice Millie said, "I can't see."

Doctor Elliston responded in German. "Can you see anything?"

Still speaking in German, "Could I have some water? I see light and color. I can tell there is movement because the color changes shape as people are moving."

"I know you are scared, but your body has suffered terrible trauma. I will have an eye specialist in here this afternoon. He will be able to tell us if your eyes have suffered any permanent damage. We will have to see."

Millie laid her head back against the pillow. "Where am I? Everyone is speaking English."

"I will answer that in just a moment. What is the last thing you have a memory of?"

"I had been taken by the German Gestapo. They put me in a prison camp. I was there only a couple of days and they put me to work in a laundry. The work was hard, and they gave me and the other women very little to eat. I remember that I got so weak I could not get up, and they left me, and I don't remember anymore."

"The war in Europe is over. Germany was defeated, and the allied army liberated the camp you were in. You are ill and extremely weak. You have been brought to the United States for treatment. You are starting to get better."

"How is that possible?"

"How is what possible? The fact that you are getting better or that you are in the United States."

"I know why I am getting better. I have been aware of what was going on but was not able to respond. I have been getting great treatment. This must be a wonderful hospital. I want to know how I got here."

"It is a long and complicated story. I will tell you over the next few days. I have other patients. I will be back this afternoon after you have seen an eye doctor. One question before I go. Do you speak any English? It would be easier for the nurses if you can, and it would help them to communicate your needs to me."

Millie spoke in English in her very weak voice. "I speak English very well, and I also speak French."

At noon, a nurse came into the room carrying a tray of food. "I understand you speak English. I hope I did not say anything to embarrass myself over the last couple of days. My name is Hope. That is the best name in the world for a nurse. I got a treat today. Vegetable soup." Nurse Hope cranked up the bed to a higher position and set the tray across Millie's lap. "Let's try to not make a mess."

"You know I cannot see. What do I look like?"

Hope laughed. "Honey, you are a mess. You look like a dried-up hot dog, but we are going to fix that. I can see remarkable improvement since you got here. Your hair is growing, and soon you will be your old self. Your skin is looking so much better, and I heard the doctor say you will not even have any scars."

That afternoon, the eye doctor gave Millie an exam. "Your eyes don't seem to have any damage that I can see. We can hope as your body continues to get better your vision will also improve. I can't guarantee that this will happen, but we can hope. Let us give your eyes a couple of months and see what happens. If you have not improved by then we will look at other options."

"What other options?"

"We will start to train you to live without your vision. Let's hope it does not come to that. We need to continue getting you stronger and hope this does the trick."

The next morning a young man with a wheelchair came to Millie's room. "I am going to take you for a ride this morning. Let me help you. I am going to place you in a wheelchair." He easily picked up Millie and placed her in the chair.

"Where are you taking me?"

"A good place. When we return you will feel like a new woman. You are going to get a massage. We are going to get those unused muscles fired up again."

"What does fired up again mean?"

"I am sorry. It is slang. It means we are going to get your muscles working again. We want you to be able to walk out of here."

The young man was right. The therapist used hot oil and gave her legs, arms, and back a complete massage. On the way back to her room she felt the wheelchair stop and heard the voice of Doctor Elliston. "How are we doing?"

"Thank you, thank you. The massage was wonderful. I don't know when I have felt so good."

"I am glad you feel that way. We are going to give your muscles a workout with a massage for the next five days, and then what we are going to do might not feel so good."

Millie was concerned. "What are you going to do?"

"I am not going to do anything, but you are going to start standing up. It might cause you some pain. We must make sure your leg bones can support you. We will take some x-rays and run a couple of tests. I feel good about getting you on your feet. You also have some bedsores that are not completely healed. Getting you up and moving should get rid of those. Once you can stand, then you can start to try to take steps. I have to leave now, but believe me you, are looking much better."

"I know what I look like. I look like a dried-up hot dog. I am almost glad that I can't see myself."

"How do you know you look like a dried-up hot dog?"

"Hope told me. I asked her what I looked like and that was her description, but she said you were going to fix that."

"When you came here your weight was about seventy pounds, you had very little hair, your skin was grey and covered with sores. Your weight is increasing, blood pressure is getting where it should be. Your hair was short grey and dried. All that is changing. I must agree with Hope. You looked like a little dried-up hot dog, and we are going to fix that. I am leaving, but remember, we are going to have you walking before long."

Millie was looking forward to walking again. "I will do my best. Will you come by and see me this afternoon before you leave? We need to talk."

When Doctor Elliston came by the room, she found Millie sitting in the wheelchair. "I am here. I am going to take you downstairs to the cafeteria and get us some coffee. It is not far, and you need to get out of this room for a while."

Once Doctor Elliston had gotten the coffee and they were seated at a table, Natalie spoke. "You said you needed to talk to me."

"Where is my coffee?"

"It is right in front of you. Put your hands on the edge of the table and slide them slowly away from you and you will find your cup."

Millie picked up the cup of coffee, carefully took a sip, and with shaking hands placed the cup back on the table. Then she started speaking in German. "Something does not make any sense. I need to know some things."

Doctor Elliston knew why Millie was speaking German. She wanted the conversation to be private. "I will answer your questions if I know the answers. I may want to ask you some questions also. One other thing. I think we have known each other long enough that you can call me Natalie. My name is Natalie."

"Okay, Natalie. Why was I chosen to be brought to America? Am I the only one?"

"An American doctor took interest in you while you were at Dachau. He found you a challenge and he must care for people. I do not know much more. You are the only one, or at least the only one I know of who has come to America."

"Do you think that he knew anything about me?"

"I did receive a letter from him, and he said about the only thing he knew about you was your name. When the Allies went through the records of the camp, they found the date you were brought to the camp and your name. That was it. You are aware that you have a number on your wrist. They matched your number to your records. Now I have a question. Who is Millie Becker Berenson?"

Millie shifted in her seat. "It feels good that I have some movement. As you know, I am Jewish. I was born in Bavaria. I lived with my mother and father in Munich. We were not wealthy, but we had a good living. I guess compared to most people in our area we were considered wealthy. My father had a large store. When I finished school, the situation with our people living in Germany was getting bad. My parents decided to send me to Switzerland to complete my education. I lived with my aunt and uncle while I was there and completed both my college degree and medical degree while I was living in Switzerland. I am a doctor but have not done the last step to get certified."

"Doctor Berenson." Natalie smiled but could see that Millie could not see her approval. "How did you end up in Dachau?"

"Things in Germany got worse. I had lost all contact with my mother, father, and brother. I didn't go home, and I wanted information about my family. I had to know about them. I secured the help of some men, or maybe they were just boys, to try to get to Munich to see what had happened. I knew that going into Germany was dangerous, and I paid to have fake papers made. We didn't get far, and I was arrested. Frank

Christian, a young man I thought was my friend, turned me over to the German police. Do you think your doctor friend in Germany could try to find out about my parents? I don't expect good news. I also need to let my aunt and uncle know where I am and that I am alright."

"I will contact my friend as soon as possible." *I wonder if I should let Millie know that my doctor friend is my brother. No, I can't do that. He made me promise to keep things secret. I did tell Tom. I will not keep secrets from him.* "If you can give us the address, we will get a letter out to your aunt and uncle as soon as possible. Your body has suffered a lot from your lack of food and your treatment. For the time being, I am glad you cannot see yourself. I don't even know how old you are."

"I am twenty-seven years old."

Natalie stared at Millie. *I guess my brother is not married to an older woman after all. I don't think I am going to tell him about Millie's age. This withholding of information can work both ways.*

That night, Natalie prepared three correspondences. The first was to the medical school in Switzerland requesting records of Millie. The second was to Millie's aunt and uncle telling them about Millie, and the third was to her brother in Germany.

Nathan Weber
Box 1223
Munich, Germany

Dear Nate,

Hope this letter finds you are doing well. Tom sends his regards, and we hope to see you soon. Millie is doing well, although she is blind. We hope as she grows stronger her vision will come back. Her weight is almost eighty pounds, and her hair is now about three inches long and has good color. I have some other information about your wife. She is more than just Millie Becker Berenson. She is Doctor Berenson. She has a medical degree from a medical school in Zurich. She grew up in a town close to you in Bavaria. The name of the town is Munich. I hope you use this information to find out more about her and what happened to her family. I have not told Millie about you and that you married her to get her out of Germany. She is going to ask and has already questioned why she is the only one who came to our hospital. What do you want me to tell her?

She is getting stronger every day, and she will soon have to leave the hospital. I am going to take her to my home. She is going to need clothing. I will use your account to buy her what she needs. I am going to get the best. You don't want to be a cheapskate with your old wife.

Love, Natalie.

During the next several weeks, Millie began to stand, then walk a few steps, and later could walk unassisted around the hallway of the hospital. It was a Sunday morning and Millie was lying in bed, thinking about what was going to happen to her. She turned to her side and opened her eyes. She could see a clock on the wall. Even though it was blurred she could make out that it was 6:10. She raised up and looked about the room. Everything was blurred, and as she continued to survey the room, everything came into focus.

Just then a nurse came in. "Today is a good day for you. You are checking out."

Millie recognized the nurse's voice. "You are Hope." She got up and walked to the surprised nurse. She hugged her. "You are right. It is a good day. I can see."

When Natalie came to see Millie, she found the room full of nurses. They were laughing and some had tears of joy. "What is going on? I know that checking out is a joyful occasion, but aren't we overdoing it?"

Millie was dressed in some clothing that Natalie had left the night before. The nurses parted to let Natalie see. She could see Millie's shining eyes and she knew. She came to her, and the two women hugged. Millie was crying as she said, "I knew you had to be beautiful, but I had no idea. You are a beautiful angel."

Natalie stepped back and looked at Millie. "You look fine, I did not want to invest too much in clothing until you got your weight back."

That afternoon, Natalie brought Millie to her home. She showed her to a room that was at the end of a long hallway. "This is your room. It has a bath and if I am not here, we have a live-in housekeeper. She is just up the stairs, and you have an intercom to her room. Here it is. Just push the large button and it will ring every room that has an intercom in it. I have marked the button which will call Alice, our maid. Tomorrow if you feel alright, we are going to go shopping and buy you some clothes. We may have trouble finding your size, but we will adjust as you gain weight. When you get tired, we have a wheelchair for you to rest in while we push you."

"How can you keep doing this? You have doctored me back to health. You are giving me a place to live and now buying me clothes. You can't keep doing this. I need to find a way to pay you back." *I have money. If I could get to my bank in Switzerland I could start paying my way.*

About that time, Tom came in from the kitchen. "Millie, welcome to our humble home."

"This is not a humble home. You could set the home I grew up in into it twice, maybe three times."

"Millie, I must give you some information. You asked me how you were able to come to the United States. I said it was complicated. I need to explain how this miracle happened. Tom, push Millie to the den and I will get us some coffee."

In just a few minutes Natalie came into the den carrying a tray with three cups of coffee. She took a seat at a small table, and Millie pushed her wheelchair up to the table. Tom also took a seat. "You asked how you were able to come to the United States. You were brought here under the War Brides Act. This act was passed by congress to allow soldiers who had married non-citizens of the United States during the war to bring their wives back to the United States."

Millie gave a half-laugh. "I am not a bride. I have never had a serious boyfriend. Are you telling me that I am married to a soldier?"

"Well, yes and no. The only way you could come to the United States was to have you marry an American citizen who was a soldier. This was done while you were in a coma. I hope you don't get upset. If this had not been done, I am sure you would have died without the care you got at Boston General. The marriage was never intended to be a lasting marriage. Once your health returns, we can free you of this marriage."

"I am not upset. I am thankful for someone kind enough to do this for me. Do you know who my mystery husband is?"

"Yes, I do. But I am not going to tell you who he is. First, you would have no idea who he is even if I told you, and second, he asked me not to."

"That does not make any sense! Why would he not want me to know who he is? Is he here in the United States? Is he here in Boston? You can tell me that much. I need to know what is expected of me."

"There is nothing expected of you. I am going to be frank. As soon as you are on your feet, you will be asked for a divorce or an annulment. Your marriage will simply go away, and all that will be expected of you is to pay it forward."

"Pay it forward. What does that mean?"

"It means when you can, help someone else."

Millie started talking extremely fast. "I don't know when that could ever be. I will need money. I do not have a job. How can I even get back to Germany? Is there anything to go back to? How can I stay here? I am not even a citizen."

"Slow down, Millie. You are getting ahead of yourself. You are a citizen. When you married an American soldier, you became a citizen. After dinner, we are going to sit down and discuss your concerns. Meanwhile, you take a nap, and I think I will do the same."

Millie was quiet during the dinner meal. She could now see, and this gave her an advantage she didn't have before. She could see the expressions on their faces, and this gave her more information. After the meal, they met in Tom's office. He took a seat behind his desk while Natalie and Millie sat across the desk from him. He looked at Millie and said, "I am looking at the legal issues. The War Brides Act allowed you to come to the United States. An annulment might make staying here complicated. A divorce would protect you if you wanted to stay in the United States, but an annulment would not."

"What is the difference?"

"A divorce dissolves the marriage. It recognizes the marriage but brings it to an end. An annulment does away with the marriage as if it never existed. I am not sure an annulment would allow you to stay in the States. You might not want to, but you may want to keep that option. If a year passes and we have taken no action, an annulment may not be an option.

That is down the road. The longer you are married, the simpler a divorce is going to be."

Millie gave a weak smile. "I could not be happier that my unknown husband, and you and Natalie, have gone out of your way to save my life, and are now giving me a home. Someday I will want a husband, and I do not know how I will ever be able to explain this to him. I may never marry. I had a boyfriend in Switzerland. It was nothing serious. I tried to get home to Munich, and he betrayed me and turned me over to the Germans. I have no idea why he did this. It was like he was working for the Germans. Everything seems hazy now. I am not sure if I am remembering it correctly. I don't know what to do. Maybe I should go back to Switzerland and finish my medical training and go from there."

Natalie spoke up. "That brings up something we need to discuss." She picked up a large package and said, "These are your academic records from your medical school. I have not opened them, but I discussed you at some length with the head of the school. You were impressive. They want you back. If they want you, I am sure our hospital and school here will want you too. You can finish your obligations here if you can pass a test or two."

Millie felt good. There was a light at the end of the tunnel. She leaned over and hugged Natalie. "How do we get started?"

Millie continued to get stronger and gain weight. She could now walk and continued to press Natalie for information about her husband. She loved Tom and Natalie but secretly resented the fact that she was not told about who her husband was.

During Christmas, she almost forgot she was Jewish and celebrated the Christian Christmas with Tom and Natalie.

Christmas was both a happy time and a sad time. They exchanged gifts on Christmas Day. Nate called, and he and Natalie had a short conversation.

He said hello to Tom and asked briefly about Millie. It was a wonderful day for Millie, but that night she felt guilty. She was in the United States, alive and continuing her life, but she had no information about her mother, father, and brother.

After the Christmas holiday, she would continue her medical training. This she looked forward to. She could start a career, have her own money, and get her own place to live. Millie knew she did have money, and lots of it, but it was in a bank in Switzerland, and she did not know how she was going to get there.

By January, Millie was able to walk without a walker or cane and was getting stronger every day. As the weather got better, she started each morning with a brisk walk, and it was not long until she was jogging. She was now training at the hospital, and everyone was impressed with her ability to learn things so fast. By June, she was assisting with operations and making rounds on her own. The year seemed to be flying by. Natalie and Tom did not seem to be interested in talking about Millie's marriage or the divorce, and she was too busy and too tired to bring it up most of the time.

Marta

Nate found that working in Munich was all-consuming. He was working as a doctor, but he was also doing administrative duties. Early in 1946 he was promoted to colonel and put in charge of the hospital. He often thought of his sister's request to try to find out about what had become of Millie's family. He had told Natalie that he would, but the truth was, he did not want to become involved. He felt proud of Millie, but he wanted to keep his distance. Millie was living with his sister and was becoming a doctor. He did not know why, but he dreaded the day he would have to face her.

In February he was called to a meeting with a planning committee. He quickly found that it was not a planning meeting at all. The person in charge was General Callaway. The general started the meeting by bragging about the work that Nate had done. Then he spoke directly to Nate. "The reason we have called you in is to inform you that we are closing the hospital. It was never intended to be a permanent hospital. It was just a field hospital set up in the school. Looking at your numbers, most of the men who were wounded have been transferred back to the United States. I understand that you are treating some of the local population. That is good. You are building a strong relationship with the people of the area."

As Nate sat and listened to the general, he thought that he was going to be transferred to another location. Then General Callaway said, "While we are closing the hospital, we are going to open a second one. We have located a building that was bombed during the war. We feel like we can convert it into a smaller hospital that would serve the men at the base and continue to serve the people of this area."

Nate liked the idea. "What about the clinic at the base? Will it continue to operate?"

"Yes. We will need both. You will be put in charge of the new building. I have the plans in my office, and I want you to go over them before you leave."

"How many beds will the new hospital have?"

"Fifty beds and two operating rooms. We hope to have the new facility up and running before fall. An American company will oversee the construction, but we are going to hire some local construction workers. These will have to be approved by you."

During the next month, Nate found he was helping with the new hospital and supervising the closing of the old school. It was being converted back to a school and was going to be turned over to the local government.

Near the end of March, Nate found that he had not hired enough local workers for the project. He called for a driver and went to see Willa. When he arrived, he saw Albert working on the porch that ran across the front of the small house.

When Nate got out of the Jeep, Albert came to greet him. "Doctor Weber, I am so glad to see you. Willa is not here, but she should return in about an hour. I hope you will wait."

Nate smiled. "I didn't come to see Willa. I came to talk to you. Have you had any luck in finding work?"

"No. I have picked up some part-time jobs, but they do not last long and do not pay very well. I am hoping when better weather gets here, I can get some work in helping with the crops."

"That is the reason I am here. We are building a new hospital and converting the old hospital back to a school. An American company is doing the work, but we are hiring some locals to work on the project. Is this something you would be interested in?"

"Yes. I have worked in construction before the war. Just tell me what I need to do."

"Meet me in my office in the morning, and I will take you to the construction boss and see if we can get you started. I am curious. There is a lot of construction going on around here. Why have you not gotten a job? Have you tried?"

Albert dropped his head and in a muffled voice said, "Many of the people in this area know that I deserted near the end of the war, and they won't hire me."

"Well, as I said, this is an American company. We will get you started tomorrow."

For the next month, Nate was extremely busy. He either ate on the run or grabbed a snack before going to bed. Finally, he got a break and decided to go out and eat. He put on civilian clothes and went to a new restaurant which had been recommended to him. There was still lots of rubble from the war, but walkways were clear for easy access to the area. It was early and the restaurant was not busy, so he asked for a table near the window. Looking around the restaurant, he noticed that the clientele were some Americans, Swiss, and very few Germans. While he was looking at the menu, the server came to the table. She thought he was an American, so she tried to speak to him in English. Her English was not very good, and she struggled with it. Nate decided he would continue the conversation in English and said, "Do you have a good house wine?"

She paused and said, "Yes."

"Bring me a bottle, and I am ready to order." He could tell she had to think about what he said. At first, he thought he should speak German but also felt she needed the practice. He looked at her name tag. "Marta, do you need me to repeat what I just said?"

About that time a second server came to the table. "I am sorry sir, but Marta is new. She struggles with the language. We both will help you."

Marta was frustrated. Speaking in German she said, "These Americans come to our country, throw their money around, and don't bother to learn our language. I hate them!"

The other server said in a low voice, but Nate could hear, "Marta, you need this job. Be calm. Just speak slowly, and if you don't understand just ask him to repeat his order."

The other server left Marta alone. Nate thought that he should start speaking German but decided against it. He smiled at Marta and pointed at the menu. As he pointed to the items on the menu he said, "Bring me the schnitzel with potatoes and tomatoes." He then pointed at a salad, "I will take a salad also."

Marta realized that he was helping her by pointing at the food items on the menu. She thanked him and left him at the table. She returned in just a few minutes with the salad.

The rest of the meal went well. Marta brought him his check, pointed to the front of the restaurant, and said, "Pay there." As she walked away, he noticed she was wearing stockings, and one had a hole in the back. He got up and reached in his billfold and laid an American twenty-dollar bill on the table. *I guess you won't hate Americans when you get this transferred to German marks.*

In the next week things slowed down, and he was able to get more free time away from the hospital and the construction sites. Albert was now working every day, and reports stated he was doing a good job.

The following weekend, Nate was asked to come to a local church and give a report on the progress of the hospital. When he arrived, the minister asked how he should be introduced. He told him to just say he was Doctor Nate Weber, and that he was head of the hospital and working with the construction of the school and new hospital.

When Nate finished his talk, he was taken to the basement where he was introduced to various people. Once he was finished, he was sitting at a table drinking a glass of punch when a young lady came up to him. Speaking in German she said, "You tipped me way too much the other night. I am sorry about my struggle to take your order. I had no idea that you were German. Why didn't you speak German the other night?"

"That is a lot to respond to. First, the tip was fine. I thought you did a good job, and second, I am not German, I am an American working in Germany, and third I thought you needed the practice with your English."

She laughed. "I need a lot of help."

"You know what I want, and this place does not have it. I want a cup of coffee. There is a small coffee shop just across the street. Will you join me?"

Marta thought for a moment and then said, "Why not."

As Marta and Nate walked across the street, she wondered if she had made a wise decision. The coffee shop was in a building that had been spared by the bombing. She felt that he was trying to pick her up. Once they were inside the coffee shop, they took a seat, and he started the conversation. "Would you like to have our conversation in English or German?"

Marta laughed. "I don't think we would have much of a conversation in English. I find it strange that you invited me to have a coffee with you."

"It is not strange. I have been here in this country for over a year and have not talked to many people or made many friends."

"Yes, but you know nothing about me."

"I know enough. I know that you work as a server in a restaurant. I know your English needs some work. I also know you're married."

"How do you know I am married?"

"You are wearing a ring. How long have you been married?"

"Ben and I got married in 1938. Our marriage was short. He was a soldier, and the war broke out the following year."

"Your name tag says your name is Marta. What is your last name?"

"It is Jenner. That is my married name."

"I notice you said he was a soldier. Is he back from the war?'

Marta sat in silence for a while. "He was on the Eastern Front. We invaded Russia. He took part in the siege of Leningrad. He never returned. I did get a letter that said, 'missing assumed dead.' That is the reason I was in the church today. They have a foundation that is searching for missing soldiers. I was there to see if he had been located. What about you. Are you married?"

"I am. My wife is back in the United States." He did not want to tell her anymore. It would sound like he was looking for something more in a relationship.

"You're a doctor. You have an education. I went to college for three years. When the bombing started, I withdrew and helped with the war. I am not a Nazi. I wanted to help bring our boys home."

"You know that I am a little more than a doctor. I am also a colonel in the army. I don't wear my uniform because I am with German civilians a lot, and I find they trust me more as Doctor Weber than Colonel Weber." Nate looked at his watch. "I need to get back to my office. Thanks for having coffee with me. I was not looking for female companionship. I was just looking for companionship. Here is a card with my information on how you can reach me. If you would like, I can search for your missing husband through our records. We have an enormous collection of the

German records that I can look through." He got up from the table. "I hope to see you again. If not, good luck with your new job and finding your husband."

A week went by, and Nate never heard from Marta. He thought about going to the restaurant to see her but thought better of it. He was sitting in his office when his secretary knocked on his door. "Doctor Weber, there is a Mrs. Jenner to see you. She does not have an appointment, but you seem to be free."

"Yes, send her in."

When Marta entered the room, Nate stood up but didn't move from behind his desk. "Marta, it is good to see you. Please take a seat."

Marta was wearing a dress with a printed pattern on it. It buttoned up the front, and she had a sweater over the top of the dress. He thought to himself that she was attractive wearing the simplest of clothing.

Marta took a seat and said, "Doctor Weber, you said you might be able to help me. I need to find out what happened to Ben. I need to know if he is dead or alive. 'Missing in action, assumed dead' is not a closure. Can you please help if you can?"

"What records do you have that would give us something to go on?"

"I have a copy of his military information. It includes his military number, his outfit, the unit he was assigned to, and other information. I have the notice sent to me once he went missing. I also have his last letter sent from the front."

"I will do what I can. What you have will help a lot. Would you like a cup of coffee?"

"I would love to stay and chat, but I must get to work. Please help. I will pay you what I can. When should I check back with you?"

"I am not sure. This may take some time. How can I get in touch?"

"If you find out anything, just come by the restaurant. I work on Tuesday through Saturday from ten to ten. The hours are long, but I need the work, and I only work five days a week."

That afternoon, Nate took the records to a friend who worked in intelligence. Nate had met Tony Marks some years earlier. They talked for a few minutes then Tony said, "Nate, I know you didn't come out here to just catch up. What do you need?"

Nate smiled. "Well, there is something I need, but I am not sure if you can help me or not. I have met a woman. Her husband is listed as missing and possibly dead. Is there any way you can find out more information?"

"You didn't need to come out here to find out that kind of information. There must be more."

"There is. He is not an American soldier. He is German."

"That changes things. I would not do this for anybody else. If I can find out anything, you are going to owe me a round of drinks. I see you have some records. Let me have those and give me some time."

Two weeks later, Nate had a message to call Tony Marks. Late that afternoon he was sitting in his office. Marks opened up a file and said, "I have some information, and it may or may not help you."

Leaning forward toward Marks' desk, he said, "You have found something. Tell me what you have found."

"Ben Jenner was not in the siege of Leningrad. I have located a German report that weeks before the Germans were at the gates of Leningrad, Ben Jenner and two other soldiers were sent on a reconnaissance mission. Two of the soldiers returned. Jenner did not. The report says that when the other two soldiers returned, they reported they came under fire, and Jenner was shot. To save their lives, the two other soldiers left Jenner, assuming he was dead. This report is not conclusive evidence that Jenner is dead, but I would venture to say that he is."

"Thank you, this will help. Can I get a copy of this report?"

"I can't give you a copy, but I have written up the findings and put our seal on it. The report itself is not classified, but how we got it is. After the Germans got defeated in Russia, Russia captured many of the German documents. We are not supposed to know about that."

"That will be fine. Again, thank you so much."

Nate felt that he had all the information he was going to get about Ben Jenner. The problem was how was he going to tell Marta. He knew where she worked, and that would be his contact point. He did not want to meet her at work but felt he had no choice.

That night he went to the restaurant and asked for a seat near the window. It wasn't long until she sighted him and came to his table. "Have you come to eat, or do you have some information?"

"Both. Can you meet me when you get off work?"

She spoke very softly, "I get off at 10:00. Take your time eating and meet me up the street in front of the bakery. It is to the left once you leave the restaurant." She then spoke in her normal voice. "What would you like to drink as you look at the menu?"

"Bring me a dark beer."

Marta quickly left the table and later returned with a mug of beer. She took his order and made everything routine for the rest of his meal. When he got up to leave, he noticed the time was 9:50, and the restaurant was preparing to shut down. He had to wait about twenty minutes for Marta.

When she got to the bakery, she said, "There is a place that serves beer about a block from here. We can talk there."

They did not talk until they were in a booth and had ordered some beer. Nate smiled and said, "I feel like some sort of spy. Here I am sneaking to see you and have had a friend access a top-secret file."

Marta was excited. "Have you found something?"

"Don't get too excited. I have some information, but it is not conclusive. Some of the information you have is not correct. Ben Jenner did not take part in the Battle for Leningrad." He could see the surprised look on her face. "The information I have happened weeks or months before the battle. This is both good and bad information. Jenner was not part of the thousands of men who surrendered to the Russians. Your report could still be correct. He is missing."

"How could my information be wrong? It was sent to me by the government before the war ended."

"I don't know. After Leningrad, the Russians were moving east. Our army was attacking from the west. Things must have been… hard to keep straight. Anyway, my information is different but much the same." He opened the file that had the information. "It is in English so I will tell you what I have here."

"Why was it top-secret?"

"I will explain that in a few minutes. What I have found out was that your husband and two other soldiers were sent on a reconnaissance mission before the German army got to Leningrad. Only two of the soldiers came back, and they reported that your husband had been shot and they had to leave him to save their own lives. They stated that they believed him to be dead. I also found out that this report was not sent until the Battle of Leningrad was underway. I guess that is where the confusion comes in."

"I believe Ben is dead. He could not survive if he were shot while spying on the Russians. Why did our army mark this top-secret?"

"They did not. This information comes from documents captured by the Russians. The document itself is not top-secret. How we got it is. You cannot discuss this with anyone. I have checked, and you can write the provisional government and ask for Ben to be declared dead. I can help you with that."

"I guess you don't give up hope even when there is no hope."

Nate slid out of his booth and Marta did the same. She looked at him and said, "I can't pay you now, but I will."

Nate smiled and said, "You do not have to pay me. You know us Americans come over to Germany and throw our money around and don't bother to learn the language."

Marta threw her arms around Nate and hugged him. He gently returned her hug and they lingered together for some time. When they released each other, he said, "Why did we have to be so secret at the restaurant?"

"I am sorry about that. My aunt was at the restaurant. Well, she is not my aunt. She is Ben's aunt. I didn't want to explain you to her."

Nate did not see Marta for two weeks. In the second week of June, Marta came to his office. She took her seat in front of his desk. "You have not been back to the restaurant. Have I scared you off?"

"No, well, yes you have. I didn't want to create any problems for you."

"I want to remain your friend, and I have decided to not let my aunt decide who I can be friends with. That is the reason I am here. I am not going to be able to pay you for a while. I have moved and now share an apartment with two other women. They both lost their husbands during the war and are about my age. It helps a lot to share the expenses. The apartment is small. We eat together in the morning and at night. I hope to have some extra money by the end of the month."

Nate did not let Marta go on. "Listen, Marta, I don't want any more money. My parents and grandparents left me and my sister, well, let's just say I am very comfortable. I am glad I could help, and I didn't help that much."

Marta scoffed. "I want to do something. Based on the report you attained, I now feel my husband is dead. I know there is some hope, but very little. I am waiting until he is officially declared dead."

"Thank you for coming by. I will see you from time to time, and I might start coming back to the restaurant."

Marta's eyes brightened up and she was smiling. "You know the weather is really good. Let me take you on a picnic this Sunday. I will not take no for an answer. Please come."

"Why not," he said. "Where shall I pick you up?"

Marta wrote her address on a pad and said, "Eleven this Sunday."

Nate was not sure he should have accepted Marta's invitation to go on a picnic. She was trying to be nice because he was helping her. Nevertheless, he drove his Jeep to her apartment and knocked on her door. A tall woman opened the door. "You must be Doctor Weber. Marta will be ready in just a minute. She is putting the food into the basket."

When Marta came into the living room, she was carrying the basket. She smiled at Nate and said, "It is not too heavy, but you can help."

Nate noticed what she was wearing and how attractive she was. "I will be glad to help," he said as she led him to the door.

Once they were inside the Jeep, he said, "Where are we going?"

"Just drive past the military base and turn right and head north. Our spot is about twelve miles outside the city. You will love it there. It is a large lake surrounded by tall trees. We will be able to park near the water. The water is so clear, you can see to the bottom."

When they arrived at the lake, Marta pointed to a spot where they could park near the water. There was a small stream that ran into the lake near where they parked. Marta spread a blanket on the ground in the shade of a large tree, while Nate placed two bottles of wine in the cool stream. "That should keep you guys cool," he said aloud. Going back to the Jeep, he saw Marta sitting on the blanket. "Do you want to walk along the edge of the lake for a while? It is a little early to eat."

Hopping up from the blanket, she said, "Sure. Not far from here is a large rock. It is a good place to sit and watch the water lap up against the bank."

When they took their seat on the large stone, Nate was the first to speak. "How did you know about this place?"

"I came here as a child. I have great memories of this place. The lake stays cold all year round. It is not a place for swimming."

"Do you have any brothers or sisters?"

"I had two brothers. Both were killed during the war."

Nate could see the change in Marta, so he quickly changed the subject. "I love water. We lived near the ocean when I was growing up. It was cold most of the year, but you could go swimming."

"What were your favorite things to do as a child?"

"I don't know. There were lots of things. I liked going to New York City and going to the amusement park. My sister and I went to a local movie theater, and I liked the Westerns. What about you?"

"Like you, I don't know. I liked being with my friends. We would play with dolls and laugh. We had an enjoyable time."

Nate looked at Marta and he loved seeing her smile and laugh. He had never seen her like this. Her smiling face gave a completely different look. As they continued to talk, she made him feel at ease. When they started back to the picnic blanket, she ran ahead and picked up a small flat stone. "This is what I love to do. I love to skip stones across the water." She threw the stone, and it made a small splash and sank into the water.

Nate laughed at her. "I believe you are out of practice."

She was laughing when she said, "Don't you laugh at me." She picked up a second stone and threw it out on the water. The stone skipped six or seven times before sinking. Marta threw up both arms in triumph. Nate clapped and they both were laughing, and he hugged her. "I could never beat that."

The hug was brief, but he felt there was a chemistry between them, and when she looked into his eyes, he knew she felt it too.

They made their way back to the blanket, and as she spread the food, he went to the stream to get a bottle of wine. The food was simple but good.

"This has been really good. I know that times are tough for the German people. How were you able to get this delicious meal?"

"It is rather hard for the average person to get food. I was lucky. I work at a restaurant, and these are leftovers."

He helped Marta put the leftovers back into the basket. When the blanket was clear she shook the blanket and spread it back out on the ground. He lay down and stretched out and put his hands together behind his head. He left enough room for Marta but did not ask her to share the blanket.

Marta took the basket to the Jeep and without any thought joined Nate on the blanket. She lay down on her stomach and propped herself up on her elbows. She lay there in silence for a few minutes. She then said, "Doctor Weber, tell me about your wife."

He noticed she was still calling him Doctor Weber. "Marta, you and I are close to the same age, and I assume we are friends. I think you can call me Nate."

She paused before she answered. "Okay, Nate. Tell me about your wife."

"Not much to tell. Our marriage has been very short. I don't know if I told you my sister is also a doctor. Millie, my wife, is becoming a doctor too."

"Did I hear you say that you are getting a divorce?"

"We are, but not for a while. While we both agree that our marriage should come to an end, we are friends and want to remain so. She currently needs my support in finishing her medical training. While we are married, she gets part of my salary, and she lives with my sister and her husband. What are you going to do?"

Moving a little closer to Nate, "I don't know? I am waiting for Ben to officially be declared dead. I miss him. Dating and our short honeymoon was a good time for me. I guess you and I are officially in limbo." She moved closer to him and snuggled against his shoulder. He moved his arm down and pulled her close and they had a very brief kiss.

"There is no way I want to make your life more complicated." He gave her another kiss, but this time it was on the forehead. "Let's just lie like this for a moment and pretend we don't have these problems."

As they lay there, he could feel her breast against his body. He closed his eyes, took his free arm, and put it around her. *Good grief. What am I doing? I am about to make my life more complicated.*

Nate knew he should not get more involved with Marta. But as he lay in bed that night, he started thinking about her. Maybe he should not see her again. *I want to see her again.* He found he could not sleep. He could still smell her wonderful scent. He remembered how she felt as she lay against him. Her lips were soft and had a sweet taste. In a way, he felt like a schoolboy and had the wonderful feeling of a youthful crush. *If I didn't see her anymore, would I be hurting her more? She does not need any more hurt in her life.* He decided he would continue to see her and keep the relationship platonic. *Who am I kidding*, he thought to himself. He decided he would see her on Saturday. He went to the restaurant near closing time. He did not go to the dining area but instead went to the bar. As the bartender approached, he said, "What will you have?"

"Bring me your house beer." He handed the bartender a note. "Please take this to Marta. Tell her that Nate Weber is here."

After the bartender gave Nate his beer, he left and found Marta in the dining area. He handed her the note and said, "There is a Nate Weber in the bar."

Looking at the note she read it to herself. *Meet me in front of the bakery.*

In about twenty minutes, Nate saw Marta coming up the street. She was smiling, and he felt relief. He was not sure if she wanted to see him as much as he wanted to see her.

"You came. I was not sure if you would."

"Don't be silly. I was hoping you would be here tonight. What do you want to do?"

"Well, it is getting late. I thought we could go to the tavern and sit for a few minutes. The reason I came is that I know you are off tomorrow, and I wanted to ask you to spend the day with me."

"I would like that. What are you planning to do?"

"I am going to get a car and drive us to Fussen. I understand it had very little damage during the war. I don't know if Neuschwanstein Castle is open, but I would like to see it. I could pick you up at about ten. I am sure we could find a good place to eat in Fussen."

The next day, Nate picked up Marta and they started their trek to Fussen.

"I thought you said you were going to get a car?"

"I was, but the weather is so good I thought it would be fun to feel the breeze, and you can see much better from the Jeep with the top off. I can still put it up if the weather turns bad."

The trip was everything that Nate hoped it would be. They walked up the hill to the castle and were able to get inside. Once they were in Fussen they walked around arm and arm, looked at the shops, and found a place to eat. Nate could tell that Marta was enjoying herself.

They left Fussen late in the afternoon and by the time they got back to Munich, it was dark.

"Nate, show me where you live."

In a short time, he was pulling up to his house. "It is not very big, but it is home. Do you want to see inside?"

"Yes." Marta opened the door and got out of the Jeep. "I would have thought you would have lived in the camp. How long have you lived here?"

"For a while. It is one of the perks of being a colonel."

Once they were inside, Marta explored the layout. "Two bedrooms. That is nice. And you have a nice radio and a nice kitchen."

Nate walked over and turned on the radio, and music filled the room. He turned the volume down and said, "Would you like some wine?"

"Yes. That would be very nice."

Once he had poured the wine, they took a seat in his living room and listened to the music. Marta leaned over and put her head on Nate's shoulder. Nate stood up and took Marta by the hand and pulled her into a standing position. He put his arms around her and kissed her. Once the kiss ended, he looked into her eyes, and he could tell she wanted him as much as he wanted her. Picking her up he carried her to his bedroom, and they helped each other undress. In the process, they would stop and kiss, and when they were completely disrobed, he laid her on the bed and held her close as he kissed her. Her breasts were not large but firm and he lost all sense of where he was as he kissed them. Marta was moaning softly, and her hands were exploring Nate's back. As they made love their passion was all-consuming, and as they lay together Marta turned her back to Nate, and he pulled her close. They lay together quietly for a few minutes and then their passion returned, and they made love again. After that, sleep came quickly. During the night, Nate awoke and found he was lying on his back, and Marta was snuggled up against him with her arm across his waist. He had the desire to take her again but did not. *Well, what are you going to do? Here you are a married man, with a woman who is soon going to be declared a widow, with no idea how the relationship is going to go. All you can do is just go with the flow and see what happens.*

The next day they went out and had breakfast, and he took her back to her apartment. They decided to meet the following Sunday, and thus a summer romance began. While Nate did not know how things were going to go, he did enjoy being with Marta. It was not long until they were spending every weekend in his apartment.

Near the end of August, Nate was sitting in his office when his secretary came into the room. "There is a Tony Marks to see you."

"Send him in."

When Tony Marks came into the room, he took a seat across from Nate and said, "Nate, I have some news that I need to make you aware of. It is common knowledge that you have been seeing Marta Jenner. Ben Jenner has been located. He is alive."

Nate shifted in his seat. "I don't know if that is good news or bad news." He thought for a moment. That didn't sound right. "It is good news, but it adds more complication to my already complicated life. Tell me about what you have found."

"We got a communication early this morning that five prisoners of war were going to be released by the Russians. When I saw the list, I saw Ben Jenner's name. It further stated that all five men were in poor health."

"Could it be a different Ben Jenner?"

"I checked, and the serial number is his."

Nate just sat in silence and then got up and walked toward the window. Looking out he said, "Not a cloud in the sky, and yet I feel like I am going to be in the middle of a storm. Marta stays with me most weekends. I have been thinking about our future together. Now some decisions will have to be made."

"I would like to hang around and talk for a while, but I know this is not something you would want to do. You have some decisions to make. I would suggest that you tell your girlfriend. She is going to get an official notice in the next ten days."

That night, Nate went to the restaurant and left a note for Marta to meet him at the beer pub. When she arrived, she was smiling and took her seat and said, "You usually don't come on Wednesdays, but I am really glad to see you." Then she noticed the serious look on his face. At first, she thought that he was being transferred or going home. "There is a problem. What is it?"

"I will tell you in a minute." About that time a waiter came to the table with a beer. "I took the liberty of ordering you a beer." When the waiter left, Nate took hold of Marta's hands and said, "The news is not bad. It may be good news. Ben has been located. He has been in a prison in Russia."

"Ben is alive and is in a prison in Russia," she repeated what Nate just said. "My gosh. He has been in that prison for four years. Is he going to be released?"

"He is. You should get an official notice in the next few days. There is something else. Five men are being released. The report says all five are in bad health."

"When will I be able to see him?"

"He is being sent to a hospital in West Berlin."

Tears started rolling down Marta's cheeks. "My husband has been in prison, and I have been an unfaithful wife. What am I going to do?"

"First you are going to make arrangements to see him. And second, you have not been an unfaithful wife. The report you received said 'missing presumed dead.' You have no reason to feel guilty about anything."

"I still don't know what to do. What is going to happen to us? I don't have any money."

"We are not going to make any decisions until you have seen Ben. You don't have any money, but I do. When you get your report, contact me and we will make arrangements for you to get to Berlin."

Nate did not see Marta that weekend, but the following Wednesday she was in his office. "I have got the report. Ben is in a military hospital in Berlin. I have the address. The report says that there is an army base near the hospital, and they have a room for me there. I will need to borrow some money, and if you could I would love for you to go with me."

Nate hired a small plane, and he and Marta flew to Berlin and hired a car to take them to the base. Marta was checked into her room, and Nate got a room nearby. That afternoon they met with Doctor Rice.

Doctor Rice went straight to the point. "Mrs. Jenner, your husband is suffering from malnutrition, and he also has shell shock. He has not spoken since we picked him up. He will take food if fed, and sometimes he calls out for Marta. I assume that is your name."

After the briefing and with Marta's permission, she and Nate were allowed to go into Ben's room. Ben was sitting in a wheelchair staring straight ahead. Doctor Rice turned the chair to face Marta. "You can talk to him, but don't be surprised if he does not respond."

Marta kneeled in front of the wheelchair and reached out and took Ben's hand. "Ben, it is so good that you have come home. We... I thought you were dead."

To their surprise, Ben looked down at Marta. "Marta, is that you? I thought I would never see you again. Will you stay with me a while?"

"Yes, I will."

Doctor Rice got a chair and moved it where Marta could sit in front of Ben and then motioned to Nate that they should leave. Once they were in the hall, he said, "I have never seen anything like that. That is a good sign. I believe he will recover completely." He then motioned to a nurse. "Go to Ben Jenner's room and stay in there until Mrs. Jenner is ready to leave."

Nate went back to his room, took a bath, and put on clean clothes. He tried not to think about what was going to happen. The choice would have to be Marta's. Up until today, he thought she would stay with him. Now he was not so sure.

About seven o'clock, he heard a knock on his door. He opened it, and there stood Marta. "I need something to eat. The dining hall is just across the way. Would you like to join me?"

They got their food and took a seat in a booth. She gave Nate a weak smile. "When we left Munich, I thought I might stay with Ben, but if I did it would be out of guilt. Then I thought that would not be fair to Ben, not fair to you, and not fair to me. Now I see he needs me. I think it has been his love for me that has kept him alive for the past four years. I had given up, and you saved me. You brought me back to life, and for that, I will always love you. Please forgive me. I am going to stay with my husband."

"You are very important to me, and what I want is for you to be happy. It may be a little early for you to make such an important decision. You have been the most important thing that has happened to me since I came here. When Ben started talking today, I knew our relationship might be coming to an end. It has been wonderful. I have something to do tomorrow, and I won't see you until tomorrow night. I hope you and Ben have another good day. Give it some time. Let's see how you feel in a couple of days."

Somehow, he knew that this relationship with Marta was coming to an end. He did not see Marta the next day, and when he entered the hospital on the following day, he was dressed in his military uniform. Walking down the hall, he saw Marta pushing Ben in a wheelchair. She did not see him, and she was talking to Ben as she pushed him toward the dining hall.

When she saw him, she stopped the wheelchair and said, "Doctor Weber, I didn't see you yesterday. Did you leave the hospital?"

Nate smiled at Marta and said, "I had some things to do. Where are you two going?"

"We are going to get something to drink. Maybe some coffee. Doctor Weber, I would like you to meet my husband, Ben. Ben, this is Doctor Weber."

Ben didn't say anything. He gave a weak smile.

"You two go on. I am going to meet with a few people. Perhaps we might see each other later."

A few minutes later Nate entered the office of Doctor Rice. When he saw Nate, he was surprised. "Doctor Weber, I had no idea you were a colonel. Shall I call you Doctor or Colonel?"

"Just call me Nate. How is Ben doing, and what is the prognosis?"

"He is doing well, considering what he has been through. He can talk some, but he can't walk or even stand. He is eating better. With care, I think we can have him out of here in about a month, maybe a little more."

"What about Mrs. Jenner? How long can she stay here?"

"If she were an American, she could stay until we released her husband. She is German and so is he. She will have to leave in a week. There is some temporary housing I believe she can stay in, and the cost is not extremely high."

Before the day ended, Nate had everything in place for Marta to stay until Ben could be released. That night, he took Marta to dinner. He explained everything to her and then said, "Ben is going to be here for at least a month. Do you have plans on what you and he are going to do after that?"

"Ben has a cousin living in Hannover. It is where Ben grew up. We need to find out if his cousin is still alive and if the place is okay. If it is and his cousin will have us, we are going to go there."

"So, you have decided to stay with Ben?"

"Will you ever forgive me?"

"There is nothing to forgive. You will always be a part of me." He paused for a minute. "You are going to need money. Listen to what I am going to say and don't say no. I was born into wealth. I have lots of money. I have already paid for your housing needs while you are in Berlin for a month. You will need more. Things are tough. Most Germans don't have enough. They barely survive. I am going to give you some money and it will be in U.S. dollars. It is worth more and more stable than the German mark. In this envelope is three thousand dollars in hundred-dollar bills. Do not say no. If you need more, you know how to contact me. I will be in Munich for about another year."

Marta was in shock but said, "How can you not be bitter at me?" Then she started to cry.

"Don't cry. I just know things are going to get better for you and Ben. I am going back to Munich tonight. I hope we might see each other sometime in the future."

Two months later he received a letter.

Dear Nate,

Ben was released from the hospital several weeks ago, and I was not sure if I should contact you or not. Things are going well. Ben is getting better and stronger every day. We have had some good luck. The government located Ben's cousin, who lives in Hannover. He has a large house, and we are living there. The money you gave me is helping us all get through the post-war. There are no words that will ever express how much you have meant to me or express my thanks for what you have done.

Love, Marta

Contact

On Christmas Day 1946, Nate called his sister. Natalie answered the phone because she was expecting the call. "Hello, sis. Merry Christmas."

"Why Doctor Weber as I live and breathe. Are you ever going to come home? The fact that you are not here is your choice. I know you could have gotten time to come home. Tom and Millie are both here. They want to say hello."

Natalie turned the phone toward the two sitting on the couch. They both said hello at the same time. As Millie sat there, she began to think. *Is Natalie's brother my husband or at least is he the one who saved my life? That would explain why Tom and Natalie took me in. He might not be my husband, but he must have been the doctor who saved me. I need to talk to him.*

While Natalie was still talking to Nate, Millie said, "Can I speak to Doctor Weber?"

Natalie was caught off guard. She hesitated then said, "Of course. Millie wants to talk to you."

Millie took the phone. "Doctor Weber. It is good to put a voice to a name. I have heard so many wonderful things about you. Did you know the local paper did a story on you?"

"I did. Natalie sent me a copy."

"I read that you were in Bavaria when the war ended."

"I was." He knew where she was heading.

"Dachau is in Bavaria. That's the camp I was in."

"I know."

"Do you know the doctor who saved me?"

Trying to be evasive, Nate said, "Dachau was a large camp. There were up to thirty thousand men and women in that camp. I was one of many who worked there. I didn't know everyone."

"That's not what I asked you."

"Okay, I will give you a straight answer. I do know the doctor who took you from the camp. I also know the serviceman who agreed to marry you. Am I going to tell you? No! I am not! I know you want answers, and you want some closure. I have heard nothing but good things about you. When I see you, I will set the record straight."

He could tell that she did not believe him, so he decided to muddy the water. "Have you ever considered that the reason your husband has not come forward is that he may be missing in action or deceased? Let me do some research. I will get back to you. Meanwhile, I want you to have a great Christmas. Put my sister back on."

Natalie took the phone. "I guess you heard all that."

She shifted the phone to the other ear. "Look, Nate. If you have information, you should let her know what you know."

"I will, but the time is not now. I need to talk to you in private. I will call you tomorrow at the same time. Find an excuse to be alone."

The next day, Natalie and Nate were back on the phone. "I know that you and Tom think that I am an ego-driven man, and I am making Millie a trophy of a good deed that I have done. I would like to think you know me better than that. I feel that when Millie finds out about who I am, she is going to make me out to be a saint. I was just doing what I felt was right. There is also more to the story that you do not know. No one wants this chapter in my life to end more than me."

Natalie gave a sarcastic chuckle. "She thinks you are a saint now. She just doesn't know it is you. That is not going to change when she learns the truth."

"Here is something you don't know. You have been paying Millie's bills out of my account. Since we are married, and I am still on active duty she should be getting some of my salary. I set this up some time ago. It took longer than I expected and was complicated. I was not sure how without letting her know who I am. I thought she was already receiving the checks, but just found out she was not. I have worked it out that starting in January she will start receiving a check from the US government, but it will not have my name on it. She will get back pay from our marriage date. The checks will come to her, but at your address. How do you think she will react to this?"

"She will not like it. You know that she has an income of her own from the hospital. She does not need your money. All she needs is to bring this part of her life to closure. Come home, Nate. Let us put all this behind us. You will like Millie, and whether you like it or not she is always going to be part of this family. She has become my real sister-in-law. No! let me say this. She has become my sister, and I love her very much. Come on Nate! Let us end this."

Nate quickly changed the subject. "This is my last year in the military. It will not even be a year until I am back in the United States. We have discussed you taking Mom and Dad's home and me taking our grandparents' house. I need a place to send things that I have accumulated here. Who is taking care of the place?"

"We do. Tom and I check on the place from time to time, but it has been a while. A woman named Bertha Willis lives on the property, and we pay her to maintain the house and hire people to take care of the surrounding property. We co-own the two houses, and we need to split that ownership."

"Get it assessed. I will pay for your half."

"You sign this house to Tom and me, and we will sign the other house to you. What do you plan to do when you come back to the United States?"

"There is a research hospital nearby. I have already talked to them about coming there to work. I think they want me. Back to Millie. I might be able to resolve this from here. Tell her to be patient."

Natalie was right. Millie didn't feel right taking money from her unknown husband, but Natalie convinced her it was coming from the government. When Millie got the first check it was quite large, and she offered it to Tom and Natalie. They refused and convinced her that they both were from old money and had more than they could ever use.

When Millie started getting the checks from the government, she was able to figure out two things. Her husband was not deceased, and the size of the checks meant that he had to be an officer with rank.

Sometime later, Millie was sitting down with Natalie and Tom. "I can't thank you enough for taking me in. I know that you would let me live here forever, but I have found an apartment. It is close to here, so we will still be close. There is also a bus stop on the block, and I can be at the hospital in fifteen minutes. That is how I plan to get to work, but I am planning on buying a car, and I hope you two can teach me to drive."

Natalie had tears in her eyes. "I knew this day would come. You have become a part of this family. Keep your keys and still make this place your home anytime you want."

Doctor Berenson

After Millie was certified as a doctor, she was hired by the Boston Hospital and was working on the staff with Natalie. She now had an income of her own and enjoyed going out shopping. She wondered how long she would have to work before she could take a vacation and go to visit her aunt and uncle in Switzerland. She also needed to get to the money she had in Zurich.

Many of the men on the hospital staff flirted with her, and she enjoyed the attention, but she just concentrated on being a good doctor.

One night while Millie was still at the hospital, Natalie was having dinner with Tom and she said to him, "Millie does not know she is my sister-in-law. I love her like she is my real sister. I want to tell her."

Tom took a drink of his iced tea. "I don't think that is a good idea. Nate has made a request, and we need to honor it. The only reason we should not honor his request is if Millie meets someone and wants to get married. I would then say all bets are off and her interest comes first. He will finish his tour next year. Unless Millie meets someone and wants to end her so-called marriage, things will keep."

Natalie pushed her plate back away from her. "I said I wanted to tell. I didn't say I was going to. I just don't understand why Nate is taking so long. There are a couple of men who have looked her way. She seems completely healed. Her weight is where it should be. She is a real looker and extremely smart. It is not going to be long until someone asks her on a date, and things are going to get complicated. I understand what you are saying though. As much as I want to free Millie of this marriage, I will support what my brother wants."

Tom gave Natalie a sad look and said in a quite caring voice, "It is sad, but when Nate comes home, Millie is no longer going to be your sister-in-law."

Nate was spending his last complete year in Munich. He had some guilt that he had done nothing to help Millie find her parents, so he decided to try to find Millie's home. Looking through the local records, he found census records that listed Millie and her mother, father and brother, and an address. It was not long until he was standing in front of a house that had been hit by a bomb. He made his way through the rubble. He found a closet that didn't seem to have much damage, and in it, he found a box of photos. In the basement, he found a trunk that was locked. The trunk was heavy, and he struggled to get it to his Jeep. He went back to get the box of photos when a military police vehicle pulled up. "Colonel we are sorry, but anything you have you will have to put back. There is a standing order in effect that any material that belongs to Jewish homes must be left intact so if they come back, they can claim it. This has been marked as a Jewish home. We will help you if you wish."

Nate wiped his hands which were covered with dirt from the trunk. "This home belonged to Hines and Ruth Berenson. I am married to their daughter. She is back in the United States. Her name is Millie Berenson. There are papers in my briefcase to prove this. I have picked up some photos and this old trunk. I am going to take the proper steps to get it to her."

Nate walked over to the Jeep, secured his briefcase, and showed the two men the records of his marriage.

"Thank you, sir. We were just doing our job. How much longer are you going to be in Germany?"

Putting the papers back in his case, he said, "I am going to be here the rest of this year and maybe until next Christmas. I miss my family, and my tour is almost done.

While Millie was working at the hospital, she had been asked out by a couple of single doctors, but she always felt she was a married woman, and it would not be appropriate to go on dates. This all changed one morning when a man came to the nurse's station that Millie was watching while the nurse took a break. Are you Nurse Duerson?

"No, I am Doctor Berenson. Is there something I could do for you?"

"My name is Marion Smith. Doctor Smith is my uncle. We were supposed to have lunch today. Surely he has not forgotten."

About that time Nurse Duerson returned to the station. Millie turned to her, "Check Doctor Smith's schedule for today."

The nurse opened a book on her desk and looked at it. "It says he is having lunch today with a Marion Smith. It has been marked out and changed to a meeting downtown. There is a note attached to call and cancel his engagement with Marion Smith."

The nurse was just a little upset. "I am so sorry. I guess I was supposed to call and cancel, but I didn't see the note until just now. We have been busy. Again, I am so sorry."

Marion looked at Millie. "I guess you will have to make it up to me."

She smiled. "How could I do that?"

"You could join me for lunch?"

Millie smiled as she looked at Marion Smith. He was very handsome. "I can't leave the hospital. Sorry."

"Then I guess we will have to eat here in the cafeteria."

Smiling, Millie said, "I guess we can do that."

In just a few minutes, Marion and Millie had gone through the cafeteria and gotten their food.

Marion unfolded his napkin and said, "Doctor Berenson, do you come here often?"

Millie laughed. "Is that the best conversation starter you can come up with?"

He laughed. "Not really. What is your first name?"

"Millie, my first name is Millie. You know what I do for a living. What about you, Marion?"

"I work downtown at Wilson Construction."

"So, you build things."

"No. I design things. I am an architect. We are trying to bring the new buildings of Boston into the modern world. Are you a married woman, Doctor Berenson?"

"Don't you think you should have asked that question before you asked me for lunch?"

"I figured if you were a happily married woman, you would have told me and said no to my request."

Millie was enjoying her time with Marion Smith. "Yes, I am married."

Marion was caught off guard by her answer. He quickly regained his composure and said, "Is Mr. Berenson a doctor also?"

"No. He is not. The truth of the matter is that my husband and I are separated. We are getting a divorce, but he is dragging his feet."

"Maybe you should push the issue. Have your lawyer see if he can speed things up. How long have you been waiting?"

"I have not seen my husband for almost two years." *In fact, I have never seen my husband.*

"Yes, you need to speed things up. I don't want to be too personal on our first date, but I notice you have a tattooed number on your wrist. Does that mean what I think it means?"

"You said our first date. Does that mean you think there will be other dates? How do I know you are not married?"

"I am not. I was almost married once, but we broke up."

For some reason, Millie wanted to tell Marion as much as she could about herself. If she were to have a relationship she had to be as honest as possible. "You noticed my number, 90718. I wish it meant something other than what it really means. I was in a Jewish prison camp when the war ended. I was in Dachau, in Bavaria when it was liberated by the Americans in 1945."

"How did you end up here in the United States?"

"I am married to an American soldier. You can see that it has not worked out. What about you? Were you in the war? No, wait. We need to continue the conversation some other time. I have to get back on duty."

"Does that mean that when I ask you to go to dinner with me this weekend you will say yes?"

She gave him a smile. "It does. Walk me back to the nurse's station, and I will give you my number."

That weekend, Millie was like a schoolgirl going on her first date. She tried on several dresses before deciding which to wear. She could not decide how to wear her hair, and she called Natalie several times asking for advice.

Saturday, Marion picked up Millie at her apartment and took her to a new upscale restaurant on the bay. Marion suggested they get something to drink and wait for a few minutes before they ordered. Once the drinks were on the table he said, "How long have you been in Boston?"

"Not long. I told you that I was in Dachau when the Americans liberated the camp. I was about to ask you if you were in the war?"

"I was. I was in the Pacific. The war was not good for me. I thought I would come back to Boston, get married and start a family. My engagement didn't last long after I got back. I was not the same person, and neither was Rachel. I guess it was good that we went our separate ways. What about you and your husband?"

"Not much to tell. We got married and have spent very little time together. Not much to tell and not much to talk about. Are you ready to order?"

After they ordered and were waiting for their food, Marion asked, "How long have you had the apartment? The building looked rather new."

"Not long. I am the first person to rent it. When I came to Boston, I lived with friends, Natalie, and Tom Elliston. They are good people. Natalie is a doctor and Tom is a lawyer. I am looking forward to introducing you."

They spent the rest of the evening making small talk. After the meal, they walked along the bay. Millie felt better about things than she had in a long time. The following weekend Marion took Millie to a movie, and the week after that they went to a concert.

About a month later, things were going well for Millie and Marion. He kissed her good night on the first date and after each date, his kisses became more passionate. She was tempted to invite him inside her apartment but did not. She could tell he wanted more out of the relationship.

They had gone to downtown Boston to watch an outdoor concert, and when it was over, they took a walk in the area known as the Commons. Millie and Marion took a seat on a bench that overlooked a small lake. Marion put his arms around Millie, kissed her and pulled her close.

Millie returned the kiss and thought to herself that things were moving fast. She had to be honest with him. "Marion, there are some things I need to tell you."

He kissed her again. "You can tell me later. I just want to hold you and enjoy the night."

She pulled away. "No. I need to tell you now."

He could tell how serious she was. "I am listening."

"I told you that I was married and that I was separated from my husband. That is true, but there is much more. You saw the tattoo on my wrist. I was in Dachau for almost a year. When I was discovered, I was near death and given little chance to live. Natalie's brother was one of the doctors who worked to save the prisoners that were there. They decided that my only chance of survival was a well-equipped trauma unit in the United States. The only legal way to get me to the States was for someone to marry me, and to use some government bill to transfer me here as the wife of an American soldier." She smiled and looked at Marion. "Here is the kicker. I don't know who married me."

At first, Marion said nothing. Then he said, "Could you not see the man who married you? That makes no sense."

"I was not even conscious. I weighed less than 70 pounds and had no awareness of anything until I was in the hospital here in Boston. That is why I have no knowledge of anything. I don't know who my husband is. Natalie and Tom know, but for some reason, they won't tell me, and for some reason, my mystery husband will not give me a divorce."

"So really you have never been truly married."

"I guess not, but it is my understanding that the marriage is a legal one. If it were not, I could not have gotten into the United States."

Marion thought for a moment. "I know a way to solve this. You need to be the one to file for the divorce. You have the power to force everything."

Two weeks after Millie and Marion had their date in the park, she had a meal with Natalie and Tom.

During the meal, Natalie noticed a change in Millie. She was serious and didn't talk very much.

They were having coffee when Millie said to Tom, "I need to talk to you about something."

After taking a sip of coffee Tom said. "You sound serious. What is it?"

"I am moving on. Since my mystery husband will not give me a divorce, I am going to divorce him. Tom, I want to hire you as my lawyer. I know you don't do this kind of work, but I need someone I can trust. Will you help me?"

Natalie looked at Tom and interrupted the conversation. "Tom you cannot get involved in this. We need to let it play out."

This surprised Millie. *Why would she not want this? Does this mean that Doctor Weber is my mystery husband or is somehow involved in all this?*

Tom stood up and leaned closer to Millie. "I can and I will. This has gone on long enough. Millie has a life. Millie, I will be glad to manage your case. We will need a cause or a reason to file a divorce. Any ideas?"

"Yes. Abandonment."

"This will take some time. When I am back in my office, I will get the ball rolling. I will guarantee that by the end of the year you will be a single woman."

After Millie had left, Natalie said to Tom. "You told me that you would not tell Millie who her husband is."

"I did, and I am not going to do that. When Nate signs the papers, she will see for herself without me saying a word. I know you are upset with me. She is going to do this, and if I am not her lawyer, she will get someone else. You and I both know that Marion is behind this. If I am her lawyer, at least I have some control over what takes place."

Nate was home eating his dinner meal he heard a loud knock on the door. When he opened the door, a man was standing there holding a telegraph. "Are you Doctor Nathan Weber?"

"I am."

"You have a telegram. Please sign here."

The man handed Nate the telegram, and Nate handed him a dollar and went back inside. The first thing he noticed was that it was from his brother-in-law, and he suddenly became concerned. He quickly opened it and read,

> *Nathan Weber*
> *Nothing wrong. Stop.*
> *Call me at my office tomorrow at 10:00 your time. Stop.*

Nate had no idea what was going on. The next day, he called Tom's office. The receptionist answered the phone and transferred him to Tom.

"This is Tom Elliston."

"Tom, this is Nate. What is going on? Does Natalie... is there some problem with the property transfer?"

"No, Doctor Weber. This is a different legal matter."

What does he mean this is a legal matter, and why did he call me Doctor Weber?"

"Millie Becker Berenson has secured my services and is filing for a divorce."

Nate didn't say anything. After a moment Tom continued to talk. "I want you to know that she is my client, and I will do what is in her best interest. I have sat back and watched you and my wife drag this out over two years. You could have brought this to an end over a year ago. She still doesn't know who you are and how you are involved in all of this. If she knew you were the husband in question, I don't think she would have taken this action. She is smart. She is forcing the issue. I am going to advise her as I would all my clients to ask for a settlement. I don't think she will want one. I think all she wants is to know who you are and to be free to move on with her life."

"Tom, I am not worried about a property settlement. I do know that nothing I inherited before the marriage is community property."

"You are about to obtain a house from Natalie. Half of that house would be community property. I will be in touch."

Nate still didn't say anything. Then he spoke. "Wait, let me think. I have been caught off guard. I need some time."

"In the next few days, you will get some papers from me. I would say get a lawyer to look them over, and if things seem fair, sign them, and send them back. If you think things are unfair, your lawyer will advise you on what to do."

"Tom, I need you to be my brother-in-law and my friend for a few minutes. I need more time. Wait, before you tell me I have had enough time, let me tell you what I need. In a few months, I will be out of the army and back in the United States. Ask Millie if she will wait until then. I will then give her all the information she needs."

"Nate, I am not sure she will wait. She is seeing someone. I don't know how serious it is, but since she came to me about the divorce, I would say it is getting serious. I do know she has told him she is married, but separated and waiting for a divorce. They could be planning a marriage. I just don't know. Millie and her beau and Natalie and I are going out tonight to eat. I will talk to Millie then."

"Thanks, Tom. Tell Natalie hello."

That night, Millie, Marion, Natalie, and Tom went out to eat. When everyone had finished their meal, Tom called on the waiter and ordered coffee. "I have news about your divorce. We can talk here, or you can come by my office in the morning."

Millie waited until the coffee had been served, took a sip, and said, "I am on call in the morning. We can talk here. I don't mind Natalie and Marion knowing what is going on."

In a strong voice, Natalie blurted out, "I am not okay with this conversation! I don't bring my patients home or discuss their business at dinner! If you two want to discuss business, go somewhere else! No, stay here! I will go somewhere else!" She then got up and started to leave. Millie had never seen Natalie like this. She got up and followed her to the door.

"Wait, Natalie, I am so sorry. The last thing I want is to upset you. Come back. I will make arrangements to see Tom in his office."

Natalie stopped and turned and faced Millie, "I am sorry too. It's just that I gave my word that I would not tell who your husband is. Tom gave his word also."

Millie was surprised. "Tom gave his word to my mystery husband?"

"No! Tom gave his word to me, and that hurts."

"What do you want me to do? Tom is a good man, and I know he cares about me, but he cares more about you. There is so much that does not make sense. There must be more to this than even you know."

"I don't know. There is no way out, and I agree. Something is missing in all this. I just don't know what it is."

"Come back to the table. We will work this out."

The two women walked back to their table. Millie reached over and patted Tom on the hand. "Tom, thank you for helping me, but I feel Natalie is right." She then turned to Marion. "I am sorry for what I am about to do." She then returned to face Tom. "Tom, put everything on hold. I am going to wait until I can see my husband face to face for this divorce."

Tom gave a sigh of relief. He was getting what he wanted, and he didn't even have to ask for it.

Later that night, Marion was walking Millie back to her apartment. He was quiet. When they reached the door, he said, "How long is this going to go on?"

"You need to give me a little more time. This has become a puzzle, and there is a big piece of that puzzle missing. I don't know what it is. There has to be some reason why my husband will not divorce me."

"Millie, this does not have to be this complicated. Let me repeat what I just said. This does not need to be this complicated. You got married at the end of the war. Your husband stayed in Europe and never came back to the United States. It is simple. Let Tom do his job."

"We don't know if he didn't come back after the war. For all I know, he could be right here in Boston. I wish it were that simple. You know everything that I know, and I think I should know more before I continue. Please give me just a little more time."

"I have been giving you time. You said you would get a divorce. You even hired Tom to help you secure it. Then right out of the blue because Natalie got upset you stopped the divorce action. I am going home. If you want to see me again, call me and tell me you have filed for a divorce." He then turned and walked away.

"Marion, wait."

Marion turned and walked back to where Millie was standing but didn't say anything.

"Marion, I am confused. You are asking me to commit to you, but you have never committed to me. You have never asked me to marry you."

"How could I? You are a married woman. You don't wear a ring, but I am not sure you even want a divorce."

"We have known each other only a brief time. I am unsure about everything. As for the ring, my mystery husband never gave me one."

Millie opened the door and went inside. She went to her bed, fell across it, and started to cry.

That same night, Tom and Natalie had a very quiet ride home. Natalie went straight to the bedroom and sat down on the edge of the bed. Tom came into the bedroom and said, "What was that all about?"

Natalie laid back on the bed. "I didn't handle that very well, did I? I am sorry."

"I thought that you understood. Millie needs to be free of all this."

"I want this to end, but I love my brother. I am not going to betray his wishes, and I don't want you to betray mine. You and I both gave our word."

"I didn't give my word to Nate."

"You gave your word to me."

"I have talked to Nate. I sent him a telegram and told him that I was sending him papers for him to sign. I was forcing him to tell who he was by signing the divorce papers."

"What did he say?"

Tom smiled. "He asked me to delay everything until he could get back to the United States. Your outburst at the restaurant did what he asked me to do. Millie put things on hold. The problem is, at what cost? I am sure Millie and Marion had an interesting conversation going home. I wonder how much she has told Marion?"

"She told me that she had explained her marriage to Nate. He knows they got married at the end of the war, and she came to the United States, and he stayed in Europe. He knows everything."

Tom stretched out on the bed and turned to face Natalie, "So, she has been honest with Marion. She must be in love with him to share all this, and they must be planning to get married. I know she saw you get upset, but I wonder why she put off getting the divorce. She could have come by my office to discuss matters."

"Perhaps because she does not know everything and wants to. By putting off the divorce she can finish this story. There is something else we could consider. Maybe she does not love Marion. She wants more time just to be sure."

"That may be true. If she really loved Marion, she might not have stopped this divorce."

She moved closer to Tom, and he put his arm around her, and she put her head over on his shoulder. "I am sorry about my behavior tonight, but I know you are going to forgive me."

"Why am I going to forgive you?"

"Because you know that a woman who is expecting a baby has problems dealing with her hormones."

"What!"

Rosemary

Millie and Natalie never mentioned the incident at the restaurant, and a couple of weeks went by. Natalie noticed that Marion was no longer around, but she said nothing to Millie about it.

Natalie had kept in contact with Rosemary Harris so that night she gave her a call. When Rosemary picked up the phone, Natalie made small talk for just a few minutes and then said, "I need a favor. You have not seen Millie since you left her at the hospital. She is having a difficult time not knowing much about her marriage. She needs more information, but not who her husband is. I would like to bring her to Maine to see you. We could have lunch together."

Rosemary agreed and they set a date.

Millie was walking across the parking lot when she heard the horn of a vehicle. "You need a ride?" She looked up, and it was Natalie. "We have not had a chance to talk. I have four days off, and I know you do too. You want to go on a road trip with me?"

"Where are you going?"

"A small town in Maine near the coast. I hear they have great clam chowder at a little fish restaurant. I have a friend up there. I would love for you to meet her."

"When do you want to leave?"

"Early Saturday morning."

Natalie had already called Rosemary and given her instructions on how she was to handle the meeting with Millie. When they were on the road Millie asked, "Who are we going to see?"

"We are going to see a woman named Rosemary Harris. She was a nurse during the war. Her husband was wounded while fighting in the Pacific. I have only met her once but found her an amazing lady. We keep in contact. I understand she has a child, and I want you to meet her and her family. You are going to love her."

Millie didn't say anything but found it strange that Natalie was calling a lady she had only met once a friend. Now she was going to see her and her child. Millie rode in silence for a while then said, "Natalie, you called this woman your friend, and we are going to see her, but you have only met her once. I find that strange. What is really going on?"

"I have only met her once, but I have talked to her many times on the phone. I am not going to tell you anymore. I want your meeting with her to be a surprise."

Millie accepted Natalie's explanation and asked no more questions about Rosemary. During the ride, the two women told stories and giggled a lot. Millie had never told Natalie about growing up, and she was amazed to hear what it was like growing up in Germany.

It was close to noon when they pulled into the driveway of Rosemary's house. Jim Harris was sitting on the porch holding a little girl who looked to be almost two years old. Rosemary came out, ran to the car, and hugged Natalie. Once they broke the hug, Natalie looked at Jim and the little girl on the porch. "You didn't waste any time starting a family."

"No, I didn't, and I have another one on the way."

"I love your house. I would like to take a tour."

"That money you slipped me when we first met paid for most of it. We got a good deal. When we get back, I will show you everything."

Millie again was confused. Why would Natalie give a woman she had never met money?

Jim got up and let the little girl down, and she ran to Rosemary. "I told you, you had to stay with your father while I wine and dine the two lovely ladies."

Natalie noticed that Jim was walking without a limp. "Jim, the last time I saw you, you were dragging the leg. I am glad you healed up nicely. Rosemary, I want you to meet my friend, Doctor Millie Becker Berenson."

Rosemary came up to Millie and said, "Can I give you a hug?" Without waiting for an answer, she gave Millie a big hug. "I can't believe it is you. You have changed so much. You are absolutely beautiful, and you are not old at all."

Millie was caught off guard. "Have we met before?"

Rosemary was excited. "Yes, we have, and when we get to the restaurant, I am going to tell you all about it."

Rosemary said her goodbyes to Jim and her daughter, and the three piled into Natalie's car. She drove to the center of the little town, and they went inside a restaurant. It was not busy, so Rosemary told the server she wanted a seat in the back. Soon they were sliding into a booth in the back with Rosemary and Natalie side by side and Millie on the opposite side facing Rosemary.

The server brought menus, and both Millie and Natalie said they were hungry and asked Rosemary to order for them. They enjoyed small talk during the meal, and as the server cleaned the dishes from the table, Millie said, "You said you and I had met before. Tell me, where?"

"I was part of a medical unit assigned to the Third Army under George Patton. We had been together since the breakout from Normandy We had moved into Germany, and a young German boy came to the camp and said his mother needed a doctor. He was about ten or eleven and knew only a few words in English. After some debate, one doctor disobeyed orders and went with the boy and saved her and her baby. I know this because I went with him. The baby was breech. The doctor was able to make a successful delivery. The whole unit was part of this and sent several boxes of supplies including food and blankets.

Millie stopped the story. "What does that have to do with me?"

Rosemary smiled. "Be patient. I will get there. A couple of weeks later, Doctor Weber was in the prison camp and found you under a mattress and brought you to the medical tent. Your weight was only sixty-eight pounds. Several attempts were made to get you to drink or eat. I don't know where the idea came from, but one of the doctors went back to the mother and asked for the baby's milk and put it in a bottle. You took it and soon were taking water and later whole milk. This kept you alive, but you were still in a lot of danger. The doctors feared more than anything else infection. At the time you had many bedsores. None of the sores were deep, but you were covered. In addition to the sores, you had many bug bites. It was then that luck smiled upon us. There was a committee in Munich helping make decisions on Germany after the war. One of the committee members had a son who had been shot. Doctors were unsure about removing the bullet from his spine because they feared it would kill him or paralyze him. The only doctor willing to take a big chance on the young man dying or being paralyzed was Doctor Weber. The operation was a success. Doctor Weber decided he would ask for a favor and went to the committee member, who had some influence, and asked if he would use his influence to get you to the United States. About everyone agreed that while you had become stable you would get worse if we could not get you into a trauma unit with constant care. Nate, I mean Doctor Weber, had already contacted Doctor Elliston, and everything was put in motion. The only way you could get to the United States was to be married to an American soldier. There is a lot about this story I don't know. Things were put in motion, and I guess the rest is history. At this time, I was leaving the army and waiting for transportation. Nate fixed it so I could accompany you to Boston, and I also was the nurse for the committee member's son who was going to England."

Tears were rolling down Millie's cheeks. "I owe my life to so many good people." For a few minutes, no one said anything.

The silence was broken by a server dropping a dish in the back of the restaurant. Natalie looked at Millie and said, "Now you know the whole story. What do you think?"

"I don't know the whole story. Somebody in that wonderful unit married me. I still don't know who." She paused and said, "I think it was Doctor Weber. It is the only thing that makes sense."

Natalie knew that Millie was putting two and two together, but she also knew that Millie was just guessing.

Rosemary knew that Natalie didn't want to answer Millie's inquiry. "Millie, did you ever think that maybe you are not married?"

"What do you mean?"

"I didn't see any wedding. I was told that the papers were signed, and that somebody held your hand, and signed for you. But what if that didn't happen? What if that clever bunch of doctors pulled off a scam to get you to a hospital?"

Millie looked confused. "Do you know this to be true?"

"No. No, I don't. It might explain why your marriage had to be kept a secret. If that were the case and someone reported this, you might be deported."

Rosemary knew she needed to change the conversation. "Times were tough, and I don't think I would have made it without Nate. I have been calling him Doctor Weber, but we became close friends. I even slept with him once."

The two women got quiet. Then Natalie spoke. She had to clear her throat and spoke again. "Does Jim know?"

"He does. I didn't keep anything from him. Let me tell you the whole story. When the Germans broke through our lines at the Battle of the Bulge, our unit gave aid. When we reached the combat zone, we set up our mobile unit and started receiving injured soldiers. Eight of us went close to where the fighting was and started giving emergency care to soldiers who were injured so badly, that they could not be moved without getting medical treatment first. It was grueling and dangerous. We must have gone thirty hours nonstop. When we got a break, we had to find shelter wherever we could. I saw what was left of a bombed-out house and could see a small fire and made my way to it. Inside, Nate had built a small fire and was against one of the three walls still standing. We had three blankets between us. We shared the food that we had between us and used the small fire to melt snow to have water. We put one blanket down on the floor and covered ourselves with the other two. I remember I turned my back to Nate, and he put his arm around me and pulled me close and we went to sleep. If we had not done that, I think we might have frozen to death. During the night, the Germans opened fire with their artillery. The shells didn't come close, but they were close enough. We both woke up and Nate said something to the effect that he was not getting up. We both went back to sleep. The next morning, we were covered with snow." She laughed. "What did you expect?"

They all gave a big laugh.

Millie's mind started to spin. "When is the last time you saw Dr. Weber?"

"It was arranged for me to be the nurse on the plane with you and another soldier who was being transported to England. I have not seen Nate since, but he does write from time to time."

That afternoon, Millie and Natalie were quiet as they took the trek back to Boston. Natalie decided she should start the conversation. "Well, you got most of the information you wanted. What do you think? Are you good with that?"

"I got a lot more information than I had before, but I didn't ask enough questions."

"What do you mean?"

"I should have asked, who was the committee member whose son was wounded. That information would help me. Was it his son that was transported with me on the plane? I could have used that information to find out about my husband. Rosemary knows, you know, Nate knows, several people who were there know, the only person who was not let in on this secret is me. This is unfair."

Natalie, looking straight ahead at the road before her said, "You are right. There is something we don't know. I don't understand all the secrecy. I think you need to let it go for a while."

"You want to know what I think? I think your brother, Nate, is my husband."

"What makes you think that?"

"Several reasons. The way Rosemary told her story. It was like she was giving the whole unit credit and trying not to give Doctor Weber too much."

"You said that there were other reasons. Want to share?"

"For the past several months I have been receiving a stipend from the government for part of my husband's salary. I don't think that could be set up without a husband being somewhere. And then there is you. You have always said you knew who my husband was, but you never cleared the air and said it was not your brother. I am not going to ask you if I am right or wrong. This visit has given me some peace of mind."

Going Home

Millie was very content working at Boston General. She did see Marion from time to time, but she refused to make a serious commitment to him. Their dates always ended with a kiss in front of her apartment door. Millie knew he wanted to be more intimate, but she still wanted to keep her distance. She had given up on the divorce until she had met with Doctor Weber. She thought that Nate Weber was her husband, but she was not completely sure. It was summertime, and she talked to the head of the hospital and asked for a month's leave. She wanted to go home. She was granted a two-weeks leave and had three weeks of vacation time coming. She told Tom, Natalie, and Marion about her trip. The trip would include her flying to Switzerland to visit her aunt and uncle, then going to Germany to see if she could get any information about her family. Marion wanted to go with her, but she told him she wanted to do this alone.

The night before she was to leave, she had dinner with Marion. Marion ordered some wine and then said, "While you are there, why don't you see if you can find your husband and speed up the divorce?"

"I am not sure I can. I don't know who I am looking for." She had never told Marion that she suspected that Nate Weber was her husband. "If I can find some time, I will go through some of the records of the area. I am going to start by finding my old home place. I wonder if I own it."

Marion took a sip of wine. "I hope you don't plan to move back there?"

Millie smiled. "No, I have no such plans."

"Do you want me to drive you to the airport in the morning?"

"No, Tom and Natalie are doing that."

Marion was frustrated. "I hope you can find your husband. That sure would solve a lot of problems."

Millie did not look at Marion. "That is going to be difficult. I don't know who he is or even know if he is still in Germany."

"That is strange. Tom has been corresponding with him. Get his address from Tom. If he is still in Germany, demand a divorce."

Millie smiled and said, "Tom would not give me the address. That would be the same as telling me who my husband is. He has promised he would not divulge the name."

"You need to get another lawyer. Tom is not representing you. He is representing his wife and someone we don't even know. If you get another lawyer, he will give you the information you need to find out who this mystery man is, and we can move on."

"I can't do that. Tom and Natalie are too important to me. Natalie doctored me back to health, and she and Tom gave me a home. She is like a sister to me. No, I can't do that."

At first, Marion did not say anything. Then he said, "Okay. Perhaps when you get back, we can get this part of our lives behind us."

The next morning, she was saying goodbye to Tom and Natalie.

As they gave their farewell hugs, Natalie said, "Are you going to try to find Nate while you are there?"

Millie smiled. "What do you think?" Even though she had been evasive with Marion and brushed off Natalie's comment, one of the main reasons she was to find Doctor Nate Weber and demand the whole story.

"Well good luck. I hope things work out for you and you find information about your family."

She flew to England, changed planes, and then it was on to Zurich. It was not long until she was knocking on the door of her aunt and uncle's house. One gentle knock brought Jakob to the door. He opened the door and stepped back. "My, my, my," he said. "Millie, oh Millie," he said and then threw his arms around her. A moment later he was shouting back into the house. "Margaret, Margaret you must come here." When Margaret came to the door, she joined the hug and started to cry.

Jakob, Margaret, and Millie all took a seat around the dining table. Jakob spoke, and his voice was hoarse. He cleared his throat, "You know we thought you were dead until we got the letter from America. After you disappeared, a month later Frank showed up. We knew that he had left with you. He told us that you had been taken by the Gestapo."

"You mean Frank came back?"

"You seem surprised. Frank said that you and he met the two men that were supposed to take you to Munich. He said you came upon a roadblock and that you and he got out of the car and ran into the woods. He said the Germans gave chase and that the two of you got separated. He hid and said that he saw you being taken away by the Gestapo. He told us that from his vantage point, he could see the two men you paid laughing and talking to the Germans. He hid until morning and slowly made his way back here. He still lives here with his father. Is that not the way you remember it?"

Millie just sat there. After a few seconds, she said, "None of what he told you is true."

"What do you mean? Tell me."

"Several weeks before we left, I started discussing wanting to go back to Germany to find out about my family. Frank told me that his father and he made fake papers for people going into Germany. He created documents for me. We slipped across the border and met two men who were to drive us to Munich. I think they were two brothers. Their names were Lars and Abe. We made it through one checkpoint with very little trouble. German soldiers staffed it. As we got closer to Munich, we came to a second roadblock. Frank told us to wait in the car, and he got out. I remember he showed the Gestapo his papers, and they immediately looked at the car, and several men surrounded the car with their guns pointed at us. They ordered us out of the car. A colonel told the two men they were going to be shot. They asked for my papers and called me a filthy Jew. The Germans gave Frank the money I had paid the two brothers. He also took the money I had left, and I also think he was paid a reward."

"I never saw the other men or Frank again. Frank was working with the Gestapo. He created papers for people going into Germany and then turned them into the secret police. He was doing this for money."

"How come they didn't kill you?"

"There was a colonel there. I will never forget him. He called me a filthy Jew, and he struck me across the face several times. While I was there, American airplanes attacked the roadblock, and the colonel was wounded. The other Germans loaded me into a truck, and the next thing I know I am in Dachau. If they released Frank, he had to be working with the Nazis."

Jakob thought for a moment. "That makes sense. I believe that his father must have been in on this. During the war, about everyone was struggling to get by, but Christian seemed to be making money at his print shop. Selling false papers is one thing, but betraying our people is another. How did you get from the camp all the way to America?"

Millie took her time and told Jakob and Margaret the whole story. They sat in silence until she had finished.

Margaret was the first to speak. "You are married, and you don't know who your husband is?"

Jakob spoke in a soft voice. "You have suffered a great deal, and we cannot let this go unpunished."

"Uncle Jakob, what are you going to do?"

"There is a secret organization operating in our town. They are Nazi hunters. I will get the information you have given to me to them. They will investigate and take the action necessary to make things right. Let us not talk about this anymore. Have you gotten any word about your mother and father?"

"No, that's why I am here. I am only going to stay a few days, and then I am going to Munich to see what I can find out. Have you learned anything new?"

"I have not. Margaret is not healthy and cannot travel, and I did not want to leave her for an extended time."

The next day, Jakob met with a man who took him to the leader of the Nazi hunters. When he sat down with the man he said, "My niece has returned, and she has some information I think you could use." He then repeated her story.

After Jakob had left, a telegram was sent to let leadership know another Nazi had been identified.

Millie made plans to leave at the end of the week, but on Thursday they had a visit from a man. He was strange and dark. He had a heavy full beard and a patch over one eye. Jakob told Millie to repeat her story, and she did.

"So how did you escape?"

"I did not escape. I was taken to Dachau. I spent the last year of the war there."

"Can you prove this?"

Jakob did not like what was happening. "Why are you asking all these questions. Millie has done nothing wrong."

"I have to know that she was not working with Christian. I must know that she is not turning him just in to protect herself. It has been done."

Jakob again spoke up, "She almost died in that prison camp. I am sorry I contacted you. Please leave."

The man turned to Millie. "Show me your arm."

Millie rolled up her sleeve and showed the strange man her tattoo.

Looking at Millie's arm he said, "I am sorry. I remember the day you were captured. I didn't see what happened to you. I had to be sure it was not for show. They took you away, and then the planes attacked."

Millie was caught off guard. "Who are you?"

"I am Abe. My brother was Lars. We were the ones you hired to take you to Munich."

It took Millie a moment to grasp who she was talking to. "They took me to Colonel Klein's office. Oh god. Oh my. You got away. They said you were going to be executed."

"When the planes attacked, Lars and I ran into the woods. We made our way east. Several good people helped us and sheltered us. It seemed to take forever, but we were able to make it to the American lines, and we worked with them until the war ended. Lars and I have been fighting injustice ever since. We have been looking for Frank Christian ever since the war ended. We had no idea he was here."

"Did Lars make it back ok? One of you was shot. I can't remember if it was you or your brother."

"It was Lars. He still walks with a limp, but he is fine otherwise. I heard Colonel Klein say that you would be executed also. How did you end up in a prison camp?"

"When the planes attacked, a bomb hit the colonel's office, and he was wounded. The Germans then decided to send me to a prison camp."

"You don't have to worry about Colonel Klein. Lars and I found him a year ago. He didn't give us much information. He thought that Frank Christian was not his real name. He also said he was in Berlin, in the Russian sector. We have been looking for him in the wrong places."

Millie didn't say anything. She just sat quietly and looked at Abe. For the first time, he smiled.

She returned the smile. "Today is a good day. Yes?"

"Today is a good day. Yes." Abe got up and said, "Thank you. This will be taken care of."

After he left, Millie asked her uncle, "What did he mean this would be taken care of?"

"I am not sure. I know you are leaving Sunday. I will write and tell you if anything happens. When you get settled in your hotel in Munich, write to us and give us the address."

Jakob didn't have to write to Millie to give her information. Two days later, Frank was shot by two men in a passing car, and that night, the print shop was destroyed by fire, and Frank's father was killed in the blaze. Millie knew she should feel bad for Frank and his family, but she did not.

That weekend, she was preparing to leave to go to Munich when her aunt and uncle came to her. Jakob took her aside and said, "You know what happened to Frank and his father. I don't think anybody knows of your involvement. Your friend was a member of a group that is trying to make the Nazis pay for what they did to our people. There is a counter group that supports the Nazi cause, and they hate all Jews. Just in case this counter group finds out that you gave information that may have led to the death of Frank and his father, it is better that you are incognito while you are in Germany."

"How am I going to do that?"

"We have been given a fake passport for you. Use the name on the passport to register in hotels, and if you must use an ID, use the name on the passport. When you get ready to leave Germany to go back to the United States, use your real name and real passport. You do not want to get caught with a fake passport."

Millie took the fake passport and said, "Am I in danger?"

"No, I don't think so. If for some reason the counter group thinks you gave information that led to the death of Frank Christian and his father, we may be in danger. I don't think we are. We are just using a little caution."

That night, Millie went to her room to pack. She then remembered she had hidden the key to the lockbox in the Swiss bank in the closet. Going inside the closet she reached above the door frame, found the key, and hid it in the bottom of her purse.

Millie used her real passport to leave Switzerland, but once she was on the train, she hid her American passport in the bottom of her purse and pulled out her fake passport. She looked at it. *I guess I am going to be Bobbi Leah Lanter for a while. I am still an American. I like this name. When I get back to the United States, I may keep it.* She leaned back in her train seat and went to sleep.

Sleeping a great deal on the way to Munich, the trip didn't seem to take too long. Once she was in Munich, she asked for directions to a local hotel. She secured a car, and on the ride to the hotel, she could see vast amounts of destruction from the bombing of the city. She asked the driver about the city, and he told her there was much rebuilding going on, and much had already taken place. He told her that she would be able to find places to eat, and there were some places where you couldn't even see where the bombing had taken place.

Once she was in Munich, she registered at a local hotel under her new name. *I am Bobbi. I must get used to it.* She was able to find a bakery and ordered some pastries and coffee. She took them to her room and ate some of them, and then decided she would not venture out until the next day.

The next morning, she ate the remaining pastries and then ventured out. She had not been to Munich for years, and it had changed a great deal, but she still knew her way around. She hired a car to take her to where she lived, which was a short drive from her hotel. She walked down the streets looking at the area. Many of the homes that were destroyed by the war had been rebuilt, and many were under construction. When she found her home, it was a bombed-out shell with not much left standing. It was stripped bare. No furniture, no broken dishes, nothing. She started to go inside the ruins of her home when she noticed two MPs across the way. She went to them and asked, "I notice the house across the street is stripped bare, and houses that are close by are rebuilding. Do you know if I can find out anything about this house?"

The MP in the driver's seat said, "If you follow this street down to the end, there is an office for Sub Sector H. They have records of this area." He reached in the back of the Jeep and got a map. Quickly looking at it he said, "Ask about lot L16. Do you want a ride? It is about a mile to the office."

Millie got in the back of the Jeep and soon was standing outside the office. A woman who was about forty asked in English, "Can I help you?"

"Good, you speak English."

"You are in the American sector. If you need someone who speaks German, my assistant will help you. How can I help you?"

"Yes. I was told that you have information about the homes in this area. I would like to know about lot L16."

"Do you have an ID?"

"I do." She pulled out her fake passport.

Looking at the passport, the woman said, "What is an American woman doing in Bavaria inquiring about the property here?"

"It is a long story. Are you sure you want to hear it?"

"No. Not really, I was just being polite." She went to a file cabinet and pulled out a folder. "There is not much here. The lot and what used to be a house belong to Hines Berenson. He is listed as missing, possibly deceased. He had two children, Benjamin, and Millie. Benjamin is listed as missing, possibly deceased. Millie is listed as married and living in the United States. Her husband is listed as the holder of the property."

Bobbi got excited. "Who is listed as Millie's husband?"

"That is strange. It has been redacted. It has a note. It says, see attached document." The lady turned to the document on the back. "All inquiries about this document should be made to the office of Logan Taylor. It has a proper seal on it. I guess I have given you all the information I can and more than I should have. I have no idea why a simple piece of property would be sealed. There is nothing more that I can do for you. It sure is strange."

Millie was close, but far away from the information, she wanted. "If I wanted to know about a wedding that took place during the war in Bavaria, where would I find that information?"

"What kind of wedding?"

"A wedding between a German citizen and an American soldier."

"That would be rare if nonexistent. Americans were fighting the Germans, not marrying them. I would doubt that any such marriage records exist. There is an army base near Dachau. They might have what you are looking for there. Do you know how to get there?"

"Not really."

"I see the MPs that brought you here are still out front. I will get them to take you there."

As Millie got into the back of the Jeep, the driver said, "Did Miss Crab give you the information you were looking for?"

"Yes, and she gave me a place where I might find even more information. That is where you are taking me now. I don't think her name was Miss Crab."

"We were joking. She does not ever seem to be happy, and she treats everybody with a degree of disrespect. I hope she treated you well. Where are you from?"

"Boston. What about you two?"

"I am from Ohio, and Jake is from Utah."

They made small talk until they were at the army base.

The driver of the Jeep said, "Where are you staying? It is a long way back to town, and if you are staying downtown, we could wait and give you a ride. You may have to wait a long time for a bus. We would love to give you a ride."

"Thank you. This will not take long."

It was not long until she was inside the building asking for marriage records of military personnel in 1945.

The young man had her sign her name and show her ID. He went into the back and soon came back with a folder. "This is a thin file. Hardly anything in it." He opened the file and said, "This is strange. One marriage and all the records are redacted. It has a note that says refer all inquiries to the office of Logan Taylor. There is an envelope." He opened the envelope and started to read. 'If there are any inquiries about these records, contact the office of Logan Taylor. Do not release these records without written permission from Logan Taylor.' You understand that I will have to send a copy of your request to Logan Taylor's office."

"This is the second time I have come across this note. This Logan Taylor must be a powerful man. Go ahead and file your report. I have nothing to hide." *Good luck with finding Bobbi Leah Lanter.*

"He is a powerful man. He is no longer a senator. He is a cabinet member in the Truman administration."

"I wonder if Logan Taylor was here during the war?"

"I was not here, but I know that Mr. Taylor was. I have seen his name on several documents in this office. He was part of the committee that made recommendations about the occupation of Germany after the war."

As Millie left the office, she saw the two MP's sitting in the Jeep. "I am ready to go back to my hotel."

"Did you get the information you needed?"

"Yes and no. I didn't get the information I was looking for but ran across some other information." *Logan Taylor is a major player in helping me get to the United States, and he knows who my husband is.*

Millie got back to her hotel room about four o'clock that afternoon. She lay down on her bed and thought, *Something just does not make sense. My marriage must be fake. Why else would a powerful senator cover up these records? I need to find out more about this Logan Taylor, and I wonder if he had a son that was wounded during the war. I wonder where Doctor Weber is. You are not thinking straight.* As she was lying there, she drifted off to sleep.

Luck and Lies

The next morning, Millie looked at the clock on the dresser and saw she had slept until eleven o'clock. She took a shower, dressed in clean clothes, and made her way down to the lobby. There was no one in the lobby except the hotel clerk. Millie walked up to his desk and said, "Where is a good place to eat that is not too far to walk?"

He had not seen her, and he looked up. He smiled and said, "Depends on your definition of too far. How about five blocks?"

"That will do."

He pointed to the front door of the hotel. "Go out the front, turn left and start walking. In five blocks you will come to Schmidt's. Great food and the prices are not bad either. I would advise walking on the right side of the street. There is less rubble and less construction going on."

It took only a few minutes to cover the five blocks and find the restaurant. The restaurant was not new. It appeared to have been spared from the bombing of the war. It had a medium-size waiting room that was covered with dark wood paneling. Pictures were evenly spaced around the room. Not taking time to look at the photos in the frames, Millie approached a young girl greeting people at the door and taking them to their seats. "Do you speak English?"

The young girl answered in English. "How can I help you?"

"It is just me. I would like to have a seat and order lunch."

Millie saw that they had dark beer on the menu. She had not had any dark beer since she left Europe, and she ordered one with her meal. The beer came first, and when her meal came, she ordered a second. She was hungry, and she ate the meal rather quickly. She was not sure how she was going to spend her day, so she went to the cash register. The same young lady who was seating people was the same one who was taking payments from customers. She had to wait until several customers paid their bills.

Getting her change, she spoke to the young lady. "I am doing research on the prison camp, and I want to know who I should talk to."

"That is not a very popular subject around here. Most people don't like to talk about the camp."

"Why is that?"

"Many didn't even know the camp was there. Some just want to deny it ever existed, and most just feel guilty. You know, there is an American doctor who works at the hospital who was here during the war and helped with the evacuation of the camp. He would be a good source of information. I would suggest that you find somebody to help you and to escort you around. It is not a good idea for you to wander the streets of Munich asking questions about the camp. You are an American, are you not?"

"Why do you ask?"

"You have an accent. It is almost German, but I can't put my finger on it. It could be something else."

"I am from Boston in the United States. I also speak French. Maybe I do have an accent. You say he is a doctor at the local hospital?"

"He is at the military hospital, but you are in luck. He is also here."

"What do you mean, he is also here? Do you mean he is here in Munich, or do you mean that he is in the restaurant?"

"He is in the restaurant, right now. He comes here often and tries to sit at the same table every time. He is sitting in the front section near the window. He is just about finished eating. Shall I introduce you?"

"Yes, please. My name is Bobbi Lanter."

When she approached the table, the doctor was looking at a local paper. Empty dishes were on his table. "Doctor Weber," the young girl said.

Doctor Weber, She repeated his name under her breath. The two beers she had for lunch had affected her thinking. She had not even thought that the doctor could be Doctor Weber, the brother of Natalie. She felt weak. Before she could be introduced, she said, "I am getting dizzy. I need to sit down."

Doctor Weber stood up and took her by the arm to keep her steady, while the young lady pulled out a chair for her to sit. "Steady," he said.

Millie sat down and said, "I am okay. I had two dark beers for lunch, and I had not eaten since yesterday afternoon. I am sorry. I am fine now."

Doctor Weber sat back down. "I am Doctor Nathan Weber, and I assume you are drunk."

She tried to laugh but was also somewhat offended, "No. I am not drunk!" she almost snapped back.

The young lady could sense the deterioration of the conversation and said, "Doctor Weber, this is Bobbi Lanter. She is researching the camp. I said you might help her. Let me clear away the dishes so you will be more comfortable."

As the young woman cleared the table, Doctor Weber didn't let up with his digs and said, "Bring us a couple of coffees. Let's see if we can sober Bobbi up."

Millie looked at Nate, who was sitting across from her and smiling from ear to ear. She smiled back. "Have your fun, but when you are finished, I would like to ask you some questions. Is that okay?"

"Well, Bobbi, I just can't start giving you information without knowing something about you. First, who are you? I know you are Bobbi. But who is Bobbi?"

Let the lies begin. "I am from New York. I have an interest in Jewish prison camps that were created in the 1930s and 40s. I am starting with Dachau. It was the oldest camp and was established in 1933. The number of Jewish people that were in this camp is staggering. It is my understanding that you were there during the liberation."

"I know the numbers all too well. There have been many stories written about this camp. Read them, and you will get all the information that you need."

"I have read many of them. They are all the same. They are full of facts and figures about the Jews. I looked at the tragic photos of the men and women who were liberated from the camp. I have seen the piles of bodies buried in a common grave. I want more than that. Every photo of the people liberated from the camp is a tragic story. I want to understand those stories and give them life. I want to understand how the people of Germany could allow this to happen. I talked to a young woman this morning who told me that many of the German people didn't know about the camps. Some knew but denied they existed, and some did feel a sense of guilt. I am sure there are stories about families who were good neighbors and friends that were hauled away to camp, and nothing was said or done. I want to understand this."

Doctor Weber shifted in his seat. "You want the impossible. I live here and I don't understand it. Why are you doing this type of research? Do you write for a magazine?"

"No. I am a freelance writer. If I can't sell my story, I will consider turning it into a book. Doctor Weber, how long have you been here?"

"A little over three years. I doctored many of the Jewish people in the camp. I helped carry some of the bodies to their graves, and I saw the gas chambers and ashes that remained of the many who were put to death. You are asking that I relive this. This is not something I want to do, because I relive it every time I go to that camp."

"You said you have been here for over three years. Have you been home in that time?" She already knew the answer.

"No, and don't ask why. I don't know why. My sister, who I love very much, asked me the same question and all I can tell her is soon. Well, soon is almost here."

"Does that mean you are going home?"

"I have done enough here, and unless I sign up for another four years, and I don't intend to, I plan to be home by Christmas. Where is home to you?"

More lies. "I thought I told you. I am from New York, City." *Why did I say New York, I have never even been to New York, City.* "Have you been to New York?"

"I have. I have been there many times. My grandfather and father had businesses there. Where do you live in the city?"

Good grief, he is going to know a hell of a lot more than I know about New York. Millie changed the subject. She asked him to pass the sugar even though she did not use sugar in her coffee. "What are they planning to do with the camp?"

"Not sure. I don't think they will completely take it down. This is something that we don't want the world to forget. I will never forget it, but I was here. I saw the decaying bodies of men and women. I can't get the smell of the camp out of my memory. I remember picking up the living, and what I would refer to as the living dead, and trying to not hurt their frail bodies. This is what you have read about. You want to know about what it was like to be in that camp. I think what you are trying to do is impossible. The only way you could know what it was like to be in a prison camp is to have been in a prison camp."

Millie didn't say anything. She knew what it was like. Just for a moment, she had memories of her life in the camp. She closed her eyes and looked down as she tried to push the memories from her mind. She also knew that she was safe and now had a comfortable life in Boston. She thought to herself, *Go home, Millie. Let go of things.* No. She could not do it. While she was there, she needed reasons to visit the camp, and her ruse would have to do. She had contacted a man who could open many doors for her.

Nate watched as Bobbi sat there in what seemed like a daze. Then he broke her spell when he said, "You look like you are lost in your thoughts. Do you want to share what you were thinking about?"

Millie leaned forward in her chair, "I was thinking about life in the prison camp, and I think I can understand. I would like to know of the lives they had before they were brought to the camp."

"I have to get back to the hospital. I am only going to be in my office for a half-day tomorrow. Come by. I have someone I want you to meet."

"Yes. I will. Thank you so much. Where is your office?"

He pulled out a pen and quickly wrote down the address and how to get there. "It is too far to walk. If you hire a car, just show the driver the address and he will know the way."

"You have been very kind," and then she said in a flirting tone. "Thanks for sobering me up."

Nate got up from his chair, and laid some money on the table. "That should more than cover two cups of coffee. How are you going to spend the rest of your day? You know that it would help if you spoke German. Do you speak German? I noticed you have a little accent."

She decided she would not tell him about being German. *If he does not know I speak German, I might get even more information.* "I speak a little French. I am going to visit the city. What I have seen is intriguing."

"You speak French. That might help a little. We are not far from Switzerland. Lots of people there speak French, but there are many people here who speak English. I think you will be good. I will see you in the morning."

Millie and Nate left the restaurant together but took opposite directions on the street. As she walked away, she thought, *So this is Doctor Nate Weber. He and Natalie look nothing alike.* He was taller than she expected, and she liked him. He was also extremely good-looking. She started smiling. *You are not here looking for a husband. You are here looking for your husband.*

As Millie walked the streets, she stopped and asked questions about the city, and she again became German. There were several new buildings, some complete and some under construction. There were still piles of rubble from the bombing. She had told Nate she didn't speak German, but she started putting it to use. She enjoyed talking to people, and because she spoke German with the accent of the area, most were willing to talk to her. Many wanted to ask her questions, but she was able to defer most of them. During the afternoon she found out that many had lost family members when the city was bombed in April of 1944. Once, she even thought that her parents might have been killed in the bombing, but she quickly dismissed the idea. She found out that over eighty thousand homes had been destroyed.

Late in the afternoon, she found her way back to her childhood home. About four houses up the street and on the opposite side was a house that people were living in. As she started to leave, she saw an old woman coming out of the house. She greeted her and said, "Were you living here during the war?"

"Oh yes, my dear. It was a terrible time. We were lucky. Bombs fell all around us, but none struck our house."

"It must have been terrible. Did you hide in the basement?"

"No. We were not even here. We had already been arrested."

"So, you are Jewish?"

A look of concern came on the old lady's face. "You know this is a Jewish community. We were in luck and were able to get our homes back after the war. Most Jews who came back after the war found that their homes had been taken over by German families, and they have not had any luck getting their homes back. To answer your question, yes, I am Jewish. Do you hate Jews?"

Millie smiled. She pushed her coat sleeve up and exposed the number tattooed on her arm. "No, I don't hate Jews, and I don't hate Germans, but I hate the ones who put me in that camp. She studied the old woman's face. Are you Mrs. Rosenburg?"

"Do you know me?"

"I lived in the bombed-out house down the street. My mother and father were the Berenson's."

"You are Millie. You can't be. You have changed so much." She came to Millie and hugged her. "I am so glad you have come home. You were gone so long, and we thought you were dead. Where have you been all this time?"

"I left here over ten years ago. Father and Mother saw that things were getting worse, and they sent me to live with my aunt and uncle in Switzerland. I lived in Switzerland during most of the war."

"But you were in a prison camp. What happened?"

"I made a mistake. I came back to find my family and was arrested. Do you know what happened to them?"

"No. They were not here when the German police rounded us up and took us away. They may have been in hiding. I just don't know. Come inside and eat with us. You don't need to be on the streets after dark. There is not a lot of traffic in this area, and it is getting late. You will not be able to find a car. We will put you up and you can leave when it is light in the morning."

"You are right. Are you sure it will be okay to stay here during the night? I don't want to impose."

"Impose? You are not going to impose. I want to know all about you and what you have been doing after the war."

Millie agreed and went inside and met the rest of the family. At one time she had thought she had made a mistake coming back to Bavaria, and now the lies she had told Nate were becoming a reality. She suddenly wanted to see the war from both sides. Tonight, she would be Millie Becker Berenson while she was at the Rosenburg's, but in the morning she would become Bobbi Leah Lanter. She and the family talked until almost midnight, and she gained an understanding of what it was like to be a Jew living in pre-war Germany, and what it was like during the war.

The Rosenburgs put her in a small upstairs bedroom for the night. She felt good and immediately went to sleep.

Before she went to sleep, Millie had the feeling she was back in her bed in the home of her parents. As she closed her eyes, a dream came. *She was walking through a large gate made of barbed wire. Two guards were taking her into the prison camp. She saw a sign above the gate: "Work hard and you shall be set free." She reached up and touched her face and could still feel the pain from where she had been struck by Colonel Klein. Thinking of the pain, she was not watching her step, and she lost her footing and fell. As she started to get up, one of the guards kicked her down again. She had fallen into some gravel, and her hands were cut. She did not attempt to get up a second time, and she felt the two guards grab her by her arms and pull her to her feet.*

She woke up and could tell she had not been asleep very long. *It was only a dream*, she said to herself, and she turned to her side and started thinking about Doctor Weber. She felt funny calling him Doctor Weber. She often talked about him with Natalie, and they referred to him as Nate. *Perhaps I should tell him who I am.*

She went back to sleep, and a second dream came. Most of the time she barely remembered dreaming, but this one seemed so real. *She was in a stalag lying on a mattress. She was cold, and she got under the mattress to try to keep warm. She could barely move, and she felt like she lay there for a long time. In the distance, she could hear people shouting, and then it got quiet. She was at peace. Then she felt the mattress move and again she felt cold. Someone was picking her up. She could feel this person walking and carrying her. She heard a voice. "Get me some blankets and a stretcher." The voice was in English. She could feel herself being laid down and covered with blankets. The blankets were clean, and she felt warm.*

Then she woke up. It was morning. She didn't want to move. *Was that a dream or was that what happened to me when I was rescued from Dachau? Was that Doctor Weber carrying me out of the camp?* Then she heard a voice from downstairs. "Millie come down. Breakfast is ready."

When Millie came down the Rosenburgs were already taking their seats at the table. The breakfast was simple. Dark bread with butter and jelly and strong coffee. "David is going to take you back to your hotel when you are ready to go, but I hope you will spend the morning with us."

"I need to get back to my hotel. I am going to meet with Doctor Weber, and I hope to find information about Mother, Father, and Benjamin."

"I hope the information is good, but I don't have a lot of faith that you will find out anything. We have been looking for information about my sister and her family but have found nothing. Perhaps you will have better luck."

The lies she had told Doctor Weber about doing research had become her mission while in Bavaria. By doing this she should find out about her parents and Doctor Weber could open some doors she would never be able to get through.

The Rosenburgs invited Millie to stay with them while she was there, but she told them she needed to get back to Munich to continue her quest for information. "I am going to leave my address where I live in the United States with you. I am currently traveling under a different name. If anyone should happen to ask about me, don't share this address with anyone until you are sure I am back in America. If you should need to contact me while I am here, I am staying at the City Hotel and I am registered under the name Bobbi Leah Lanter. Don't ask me why. It is a long story."

Mrs. Rosenburg looked puzzled. "How will we know when you are back in the United States?"

"As soon as I get back, I am going to write to you."

Back to Dachau

By ten o'clock she was in her room. She quickly cleaned up, changed clothes, and made her way to the hospital. It was after eleven when she entered Doctor Weber's office. She was greeted by an assistant who asked her what she needed. She said she had an appointment.

The lady asked her name and looked at her appointment book. "Your name is not listed."

"We met at a local restaurant yesterday, and he told me to just drop by. Is he here?"

"Yes. Let me check." She got up, left the room, and quickly returned. She was followed by Doctor Weber. He was not wearing a uniform but was dressed in civilian clothing. "Bobbi, it is good to see you again. I thought you might be here earlier."

"You told me that you were only going to be in your office for a half-day, so I figured I might buy you lunch today."

"A free lunch. What is that going to cost me?"

"A lot of information. Where do you want to eat?"

"There is a wonderful place in the older part of town. It is too far to walk. Carol, would you have a Jeep sent around?"

Forty minutes later they were in the heart of the old town. They drove around for a few minutes, and Nate pointed out some of the historical sites. Many were under construction. She didn't tell him that she knew more about the area than he did. Once when he made a turn, she recognized the name of a street they passed. Her family's store was on that street. *I wonder what happened to it.* They went down a side street and found a small hole-in-the-wall restaurant. They took a seat and were given menus.

"What is good here?"

127

"Everything. Do you trust me? Let me order for both of us." He called over the waiter and said, "We will have the Bavarian pot roast, potato salad, and red cabbage, and bring us two of your house beers."

"Are you going to try to see if I will get intoxicated again?"

"So, you admit you had too much to drink yesterday."

Millie smiled at Doctor Weber. She felt so relaxed around him. She understood this was because she and Natalie had talked about him, but he seemed relaxed around her, and he did not know her. "No. I had two strong German dark beers on an empty stomach. Today I have had a big breakfast, so it will not happen today."

"You will like the beer I ordered. It is brewed right here in Munich. Did you get to see much of the town yesterday afternoon?"

"No. I went to a residential section. I am amazed at how much of the city is being rebuilt. I could even see it on the ride here."

"We Americans can't take all the credit. Munich was trying to rebuild even before the war ended. The real debate came on rebuilding or restoring. I think there was a compromise. The old section here is being restored. Other areas are going to be more modern. I am going to be your guide today. You will see lots of rebuilding and lots of restoration."

During the meal, Millie and Nate enjoyed the idle conversation. Nate liked to joke a lot and kept asking her about New York, which she was able to deflect and bring the conversation back to him. "Doctor Weber, tell me about your family."

"Well, first if we are going to spend some time together, you have to stop calling me Doctor Weber. My name is Nathan. My friends call me Nate. Please call me Nate."

She laughed, "Am I your friend, Doctor Weber? We just met a day ago."

"I hope so, Bobbi. I enjoy talking to you. When I get back to Boston, I am going to come to New York and look you up."

"That would be nice, Nate." *It would be nice to see Nate again back in the United States, but that can't happen if I am masquerading as Bobbie Lanter. Maybe I should just tell him who I am. Surely, he would accept me as I am. What if I am wrong? There is a small chance he is not my husband. The longer I play this game the harder it is going to be to get out of it.*

When the meal was finished, he insisted on paying the bill. "A gentleman does not let a lady pay," he said.

128

"Then I am going to spend the rest of my time in Bavaria with you. It will save me money."

He looked at her and smiled. *I would gladly pay for every meal just to spend more time with you.* He had not been attracted to very many women since he was in Germany except for Marta. When he first came there, he was too busy to date, and later the women he had contact with were not there very long. Just for a moment, he thought of Marta, and then he pushed her out of his mind.

As they got into the Jeep, she said, "Where are we going first?"

"We are going to Dachau. Dachau was opened in 1933. It is estimated that over two hundred thousand came through this camp. This is not going to be easy. We promised the prisoners that were liberated here that we would never let the world forget what happened here. I am not sure anyone who was not a prisoner in that camp can understand. But that is our first stopping point."

Millie thought to herself, *I understand this all too well.* She didn't want to go to Dachau. But she had no choice. There was information she needed, and Dachau was the only place she could get it. Besides, she had told Nate she was researching prison camps. She wanted to learn about and get to know Nate. She was almost one hundred percent sure that Nate was her unknown husband, but she had to be sure. She thought that she should say she would prefer just seeing the city and talking to people, but this would give her a chance to see some of the records. Maybe her mother, father, and brother had been there too.

On the way to Dachau, she was quiet. She broke her silence and said, "How far is it to Dachau?"

"It is a short trip of only about forty minutes. When we arrive, we will have to show some identification to get in. Your passport is all you will need." She wondered if she could get into trouble showing her false identification. Once inside the gate, she asked him to stop.

She looked at the camp and was surprised at the size. It was not like she remembered it. Above the gate was a sign, "Arbeit macht frei." Work and you shall be free. She thought back to the day she first saw the sign. She remembered the long days in the laundry with the other women and the little food she was given. She had a memory. *It was a sweltering day, and the steam and hot water were making the working conditions almost unbearable.*

129

The women who worked in the laundry didn't get to know each other because they were not allowed to talk very much, and they did not stay together at night. They washed the clothing of the guards, but she had noticed they also had clothing from civilians, and she concluded they must be doing laundry for some of the townspeople. That day a woman who was working in the laundry passed out from the heat and was weak from lack of food. Two guards came in, and one kicked her in the side and told her to get up. The woman did not respond, so they grabbed her by the feet, drug her out, and threw her into the back of a truck with several other bodies.

Millie tried to push the memory out of her mind. She shifted in her seat to face Nate. "I know that you have been here many times, but what do you remember seeing when you first came here?"

"It was not what I saw that I remember so much, although I do remember what I saw. What I remember most is the smell. People were lined up along the fence looking out at our troops, but you could smell death, thousands of rotting bodies. Many of the German guards were killed when we liberated the camp. Most were killed by American soldiers, but some were killed by the prisoners themselves when they found out the camp was going to be liberated. I am sure that the prisoners thought that they were going to be set free immediately, but that is not what happened. There was much that had to be done before they could be moved. After we arrived and liberated the camp, many prisoners continued to die. We saved as many as possible. We had no place to take them. I am going to take you over to the main office. There are records of the camp and some photos you need to see."

Inside the office, they were greeted by a young soldier who was excited to talk about the records of the camp. Some photos were displayed, but he pointed out there were more if they wanted to see them.

"We have two sets of records about the people who were here. The Germans kept good records. We have a good idea of who was here until the last of the war. Most of the original records have been sent back to the United States, but we do have a good list. Are you looking for someone in particular?"

"No. I am just trying to get a better understanding of the camp."

About that time a lieutenant came into the room. "Captain Peters said he would like to see you while you are here. He saw you drive in."

Nate turned to her and said, "He is an old friend. I need to go by and say hello. Will you be okay here for a few minutes?"

"Yes, of course, you go ahead."

The young clerk put the records he had on a table for Millie to see. "These records are not complete. As the allied armies came toward the German border, they started moving prisoners out of the camps that were near the front and moving them further west. This was not a good time to be a Jew. We know that if you were too weak to make the trip, you were shot along the way. We know of one story where 7,000 women were moved west. Seven hundred were shot on the way, and the rest were killed after they had made the trip."

He says that story so matter of factly. Seven thousand women being killed is not so just a matter of fact. Seven thousand women were wives, daughters, and mothers. I could have very easily been one of those women.

She was left alone in the room, and she started to look at the extensive list of people who were known to have been in the camp. There was a lengthy list of Berensons on the list, but her name stood out. Most of the lines on the list included names, birthdays, date of arrival, last known residence, and prison numbers. She rolled up the long sleeves she used to cover her tattoo and looked and looked at her number, 90718. Just for a moment, she let her mind drift back to the days she spent at the camp. She gritted her teeth and pushed the thoughts from her mind and again focused on the list. Her name only had three entries. Her name, prison number, and date. She began to look at the other names, hoping to find information about her mother and father but did not see their names, but then she saw it, Benjamin Berenson. Her brother was also in this camp. Her heart began to race. She called for the soldier who was in charge, who was in the next room sitting at his desk.

"You need something?"

She struggled to get her words out. "Is there any record of what happened to the prisoners who were liberated from the camp?"

"We don't have a complete file and will not for a while. We may never know what happened to all. There is some discussion on whether those files should be private." He walked over and looked at the records. "I can tell you this. If the name has a dot next to it, that means the prisoner was executed."

Millie closed her eyes. She remembered the dot next to her brother's name. She could not contain her feelings anymore. She walked outside the office. She had held out little hope that her brother was still alive, but seeing his name on the records and confirming that her brother had been put to death was almost more than she could bear. She could not control herself, and tears began to flow. Then she felt someone take her in their arms and hold her close.

Nate gently said, "It is exceedingly difficult to see name after name of the people who were in this hell hole. Most people who come here and see the list only see the names and don't connect those names to real people. Just seeing the impact of the volume of people in these records is overwhelming. You are a very caring person. It is okay to weep for them, the ones that died waiting for freedom and the ones who were executed. The fact that you are crying means you have feelings for these people. Every time I come here; I want to cry."

After a couple of minutes, she got control and said, "Can we leave? I can't stay here anymore."

They left the camp and started back to Munich. Millie was quiet.

"There is a road up here that turns to the right and about a mile up that road is a small village. It has the most beautiful church. Is it okay to stop for a few minutes? I know it is way too early to eat, but we might get something to drink and a snack later."

Millie had trouble finding her voice. "Yes. That will be fine."

When they stopped the Jeep in front of the church, Millie looked at the church sign. "This is a Catholic church. I would have thought most of the churches would have been protestant. Are you a Catholic?"

Nate opened the door of the Jeep. "I am afraid that I am not much of anything. Father Anderson has been trying to get me to come to this church, and I have made a couple of visits, but I am not a member. I see the good the churches do, but I have trouble with my faith. There must be something much greater than me, but how could a God let the world destroy fifty million people? What about you?"

She did not give him an answer. She simply said, "I have not been to a house of worship for years. I take that back. I did go to church with my friends at Christmas."

Just inside the door of the church a priest greeted them. He spoke to Nate in German. He was thanking Nate for his contributions to the church. Millie found this strange because he had just told her he was not a man of faith.

Nate handed him some money, and they walked into the sanctuary and took a seat five pews from the front. Nate said in a very soft voice, "I like coming here. This church is wonderful. It was not hit by any bombs during the war. It is several hundred years old. You can close your eyes and forget everything that is wrong with this world, or if you use your imagination, you can go back in time."

Millie leaned her head over on Nate's shoulder and said, "It is a shame we can't stay here forever. In just a few minutes we have to leave and face a world where everything is not right."

"I know. Let's just take advantage of this peaceful setting while we can, and then we will leave and try to make this a better world. You will feel much better when we leave. I know I always do. One thing I have found out while I have been living here is that there are still a lot of good people in the world."

"Didn't you know this before you came to Germany?"

"Not really. I never even thought about it while I lived in Boston. My sister and I had money, and we lived high on the hog. We took in movies, went to dances, and were unaware of the world and what was going on. Don't get me wrong, we were very aware of Hitler and what was going on in Europe, but like most Americans, we saw it as a European problem. The war changed all that. When I came to Europe, I first thought the world must be full of evil people. But as our outfit moved deeper into the interior of France and later into Germany, I could see that most people were just good people caught up in a terrible war." He closed his eyes and just sat quietly.

They stayed for about a half-hour. "Thanks for stopping here. You were right. I do feel much better," Millie said. I don't want to be nosy, but I saw you give the priest some money. You said you didn't belong to this church, but you seem to be supporting it."

He smiled. "I didn't give all that much. The church is building a playground. It is about finished. I would rather give a few dollars than give my time to construction."

At the front of the church, Nate stopped to say goodbye to the priest. "Nate, Willa is here. I didn't tell her you were here, but I am sure she would like to see you."

"I would like to see her, too. Where is she?"

"She took Nata over to the playground. Once you step outside, I am sure you will see her."

As they approached the playground, the woman and the little girl came to greet them.

"Willa, it is good to see you. How is the rest of the family?"

"Everybody is fine. Albert's job is going well, and the three children are in school, but not today. They are spending time here at the church."

About that time the priest came up and said, "Doctor Weber I hate to impose, but one of our workers has cut her hand. Would you mind looking at it?"

"Not at all. Willa, would you keep my friend company while I check on the injured."

After Nate left, Willa said, "We were not introduced. My name is Willa, and you are?"

"My name is Bobbi. I am visiting from the United States. Your English is exceptionally good."

"Thanks, but I notice you have a German accent."

As she was growing accustomed to doing, Millie deflected the comment with a question. "How do you know Nate?"

"Right at the end of the war, I was having a difficult birth. My baby was breech Doctor Weber came from the American field hospital and was able to save me and little Nata. How do you know Doctor Weber?"

So, Willa is the woman in Rosemary's story. "I have only known Nate for a few days. But I can tell he is a wonderful doctor and a good man." She had the urge to hug Willa, but instead said, "May I hold Nata?"

"Yes. Here, take her. She is quite a handful."

Nata was not bashful. She took right to Bobbi and stayed with her until Nate returned.

As Bobbi was holding Nata, she asked, "Were you here when they liberated the camp?"

"I was. Why do you ask?"

"I am researching the camp. I am just trying to put things together."

"I don't know much. You can get much more information from Nate."

"I have heard that there was a Logan Taylor here when the camp was liberated. Do you know if that is true?"

"As I said, I don't know much, but I do know that Nate operated on his son and possibly saved his life."

More clues falling into place.

About that time Nate returned. "That was not too bad. It only required a couple of stitches."

They stayed a few more minutes with Willa and Nata, and then Nate looked at his watch. "It is almost fifteen hundred hours. Let's get back to Munich."

Once they were on their way, Millie asked, "I wonder if you were in a prison camp, is that where you stayed or could you have been moved to another camp? I was told by the lieutenant that some of the prisoners were moved to other camps. Do you know if this was true?"

"Yes, many people ask that question. It is strange, but prisoners were moved from one camp to another. As the war was ending many of the prisoners were moved east. You must remember that the prisoners were slave laborers. They were moved sometimes where they were needed. It was not the same for prisoners of war. They were given a choice to work or not work. Many chose to work because they were offered more food and better treatment. This was not the case for the Jewish prisoners."

Millie had always felt in her heart that her brother and parents were dead, but she had held hope that they were somewhere alive. She now knew that her brother did not survive, and it gave her some closure.

"It is too late today, but I know a German family. I am going to talk to them and see if they want to meet you. I told you about them at the restaurant. I will tell them that you are looking for a German perspective about the war and Hitler and the Jewish people and see if they will talk to you. I don't know if they will or not."

"That would be fine." She said to herself, *The more I know him, the more I like him. What will he think when he finds out that he is married to me? That is, if he is married to me?*

"I am going to drop you off at your hotel, and I am going to go and clean up and change clothes. If it is okay, I will come back, pick you up and wine and dine you tonight."

"You don't have to do that. You have been very generous with your time." The truth of the matter was she was hoping to spend more time with him.

"I am not doing it for you. I am doing it for me. I like you. I like you a lot. I like spending time with you, and I want to get to know you better."

Millie knew that Nate was going to ask all kinds of questions about her, and she was not sure how she could answer them without telling him who she was. She should have refused to go out with him, but she liked him too much to say no.

As they sat down at their table, Nate said, "No beer tonight." Looking up at the waiter he said, "Bring us a bottle of your best red wine. Do you have a sweet wine? I would prefer it not be dry." He looked at Millie. "Does that suit you?"

She agreed.

A few minutes later the waiter returned with the wine and let Nate sample it. "That is fine. This is incredibly good."

They placed their order and Nate turned to her and asked, "Have you always lived in New York?"

Here come the lies and half-truths. Maybe I should tell him who I am and be done with it. Seems like with every lie I get pulled further in. "Yes. My parents had a store. They had a good living."

"You said they *had* a good living."

"They are deceased."

"I am sorry. Do you have any siblings?"

"I had a brother. He was killed during the war. He was killed in Europe."

Nate just assumed he was an American soldier. Again, he said he was sorry. "When are you going back to the United States?"

"Ten days. I am going to be here the rest of this week and then leaving at the end of the following week." She laughed, "I feel like I am being interrogated."

"Just one more question. Are you married, or do you have a boyfriend waiting back in New York?"

I have a boyfriend and I am married. She thought for a moment and then said, "I don't have a boyfriend. I am married." Millie could see the disappointment on his face.

Nate took a sip of his wine. "Your husband let you come by yourself on this trip?"

"You didn't let me finish. I am married, but my husband and I are separated. We are going to get a divorce. Now I must ask you. Are you married?"

He thought for a moment. "Yes. I am married, but like you, my wife and I are separated."

"Are you going to get a divorce?"

"No. Not for a while."

"What does that mean? Are you trying to get back together?"

"No. We are not trying to get back together, but just take my word, it is complicated."

"Are there children involved?" There was no longer any doubt. Nate was her husband. But why had he let the marriage go on so long?

Nate gave a half-smile. "No. There are no children involved. You are married and separated, I am married and separated. Let us leave it at that and just enjoy the evening."

Once the meal came to the table and they had finished the bottle of wine they were laughing and joking with each other. Nate liked Bobbi. She had a quick wit, and he felt he had known her his entire life, but he really didn't know her at all.

He drove her back to her hotel room and walked her to her room. They stopped in front of her door, and he said, "I enjoyed tonight. I must work the rest of the week, but I would like to spend more time with you. What if I called you this weekend? Could you find time for me?"

She gave a cute little giggle. "I will have to check my calendar and see if I can fit you in."

"Do you even have a calendar?"

"No. I will be at the little café where we first met at nine o'clock this Saturday. If we happen to run into each other, that would be great."

He took a step closer to her and reached out and took her by the waist. Pulling her close he kissed her gently on her lips. She did not resist, and he again kissed her. She put her arms around his neck and said, "What was that all about?" She kissed him back.

"What was that all about?" He again returned her kiss.

They didn't say anything for a moment. Both could feel the connection. She did not want to let him go and just for a moment wanted to invite him into her room. She resisted the temptation.

"That was thank you for today and the wonderful meal tonight. I will see you Saturday morning." She opened her door and went inside. She took a seat on her bed. "What in the hell am I doing?" she said aloud.

The next morning, Millie hired a car to take her to the street where her parents had their store. The store was gone, and in its place was a large department store that covered not only her parents' store location but the location of several other stores. Going inside she found the store manager. Speaking in German she said, "I have been out of the country for several years. I remember there used to be a store here called Berenson's. Do you know what happened to it?"

"I don't know much. I am not from Munich. It is my understanding that this area was bombed during the war, and this block was almost destroyed. Our company bought the lots from the owners or their heirs."

"Is there a record of those sales?"

"I would think that you could find those records in City Hall."

Millie was excited. She knew if her father sold the lot to the department store, he must have been alive at the end of the war. She thanked the manager for his help, and forty minutes later she was requesting records from City Hall.

The clerk was helpful. "May I inquire as to why you need those records?"

"My father owned one of the stores. I have not heard from him since before the war. I had assumed that he was killed during the Holocaust, but now it appears he was alive after the war."

The clerk left Millie at the counter and went and retrieved the records. "It says here that an effort was made to find your father and that he and your mother died in Sachsenhausen Concentration Camp."

Millie closed her eyes and lowered her head. Her voice cracked, and she had to clear her throat. "I have always known that they were dead, but it hurts to find it out." Tears rolled down her cheeks.

"I am sorry. That was cruel of me. I am sorry. I just said it so matter-of-factly. Come to my office, and I will get you a glass of water."

After Millie had stopped crying, she said, "Was there no effort to find me or my brother?"

"That, I don't know. If you can show me proper identification, I will open a file."

Millie reached to the bottom of her purse, pulled out her real passport, and handed it to the clerk.

"You are an American. How can that be?"

"I am married to an American, but I am also a citizen of Germany."

After the clerk had taken all the information he said, "This is going to take some time. Are you going to be in Munich for a while?"

"No. I will be going back to the United States. How long do you think it will take to get some information?"

"At least a month. Once it is confirmed who you are, you will be contacted. I am sure there is a nice settlement in this for you."

When Millie arrived at the café, she found Nate already sitting at his favorite seat by the window. At first, she did not go to his table but watched him from across the room. He was reading a newspaper and had a cup of coffee in one hand. She walked up to his table smiling, "What if someone else beats you to your favorite seat before you get here?"

"I just pull out my gun and make them move."

"I don't see a gun anywhere."

The waitress came to the table and said, "Doctor Weber, are you ready to order?"

"Okay, Miss Bobbi, what would you like?" he asked.

She looked at the menu. "Bring me the strudel and coffee."

"I will have a waffle."

As the server walked away from the table, he turned to Millie and said, "I really would like to have a good ole southern breakfast."

"What do you consider a good ole southern breakfast?"

"You are from New York. Have you ever traveled in the south?"

"No. Never been any further south than Maryland."

"Well, a good ole southern breakfast would be eggs, bacon or sausage, potatoes, grits, and biscuits and gravy."

"Doctor, you know better than to eat that much or that kind of food," she laughed.

"I can dream, can't I?"

"Well, what do you have planned for me today?"

"We are going to meet the Hinkles at ten-thirty this morning. They are not far."

Complications

They took their time with breakfast and later they were sitting down with the Hinkles in their home. The Hinkles were in their fifties. Both spoke English, and the man did most of the talking.

"Doctor Weber has told us that you want to know about the German people, and how we could let so many people die because they were Jews. To be completely honest, I ask myself the same question. It seemed to all come to a head with Kristallnacht, The Night of the Broken Glass. It happened in November of 1938. That was the night we did terrible things, and we did nothing to stop it. It was a terrible event, but it started a long time before that. In 1918, Germany lost the war. Most of us didn't think we had lost the war, and we didn't think we started it, but we were blamed for it by the Treaty of Versailles. The 1920s were terrible. We were forced to pay for the war, which was impossible. Most Germans were barely surviving. We wanted someone to blame. Hitler and the National Socialist German Workers' Party, the Nazi party, gave us a target. They gained power because most of us feared a communist takeover. Jews were blamed for all our problems. Hitler made us proud to be German again. He lowered the taxes and put the people back to work. By 1935 Hitler had the support of most of the German people. Laws were passed taking away the rights of the Jewish people, and we did nothing. Kristallnacht was started when a German diplomat, Ernst vom Rath, was assassinated by a Polish Jew living in Paris. Ordinary people participated in the looting. People were benefiting from the expropriation of Jewish property. Jews were humiliated. Not all Germans felt this way toward the Jews. Some were vocal and said they were ashamed to be German. Many were critical of the violence against the people and critical of the destruction of property. By

141

1938, the Nazi party was firmly in control, and most people were scared to make negative comments about Hitler and the party. Not a proud time to be a German, but we were proud."

Millie asked, "Did you live in Munich during this time?"

"We did. We have always lived in Munich."

"Did you know about Dachau?"

"Dachau was established in 1933. Its initial purpose was to house political prisoners and undesirables. Later, its prisoners contained a host of people including many thousands of Jews. You asked me if we knew about the camp. The answer is yes. By the late 30s, Hitler and the Nazis were very powerful and very popular. You were afraid to speak against anything. There was a chance that you could be reported to the Gestapo, and you might end up in the prison yourself."

Millie just sat there and listened to the finish of the story. "I am trying to understand what happened, but I don't know if I can. I would like to thank you for your time. I guess you really can't know what it was like in one of those camps unless you were there. By the same token, you have no perspective about living in a country controlled by the Nazis unless you lived here."

Millie began the think about what Mr. Hinkle has said. *I only lived in Germany as a child. I didn't see what was happening, and I was living in Switzerland during the bad times. Mother and Father protected me from knowing how bad it was.*

Nate and Millie left the Hinkles' and took the Jeep back to the center of Munich. "What do you want to do?"

Millie looked at her watch. "It is after lunch, and I am not very hungry. I need to go back to my room and write down some notes. If I don't, I might forget something. I should be through by about 4 o'clock. Can you meet me at the hotel then?"

"What do you want to do?"

"You are my guide, and I am all yours."

Millie was waiting for Nate when he pulled up in front of the hotel. Once she was in the Jeep she said, "Where are we going?"

"Right in the heart of Munich in the oldest section is a beer hall called the Garten des Lebens. They have a simple menu, many kinds of beers, and very loud music. We can enjoy the music, get you high on dark beer, and eat snacks if we want. Do you want to go?"

"Yes, why not."

When they got there and went in, it was crowded. Many of the people were soldiers, some were Americans, and some local people. People were dancing to polka music, and others were standing around drinking beer out of steins. The crowd was mostly young, but others looked to be in their thirties. It was loud, very loud. "Are all these people drunk?" she asked."

"No, they are just having fun." They were lucky, a couple had just gotten up and left their table, so they sat down and ordered two dark beers. Their table had four seats, and they shared the table with several others that came and went that evening.

They ate brats and potatoes and drank beer and danced, and she felt like she had missed so much in her life.

Time just got away from them, and when they left it was dark and a little after eleven o'clock.

Nate took her by the hand and said, "There are benches down the street. We can sit and look at the famous Munich Glockenspiel." Where they had parked the Jeep was on the way, so Nate reached in the back and got a blanket. There were almost no people on the street, and they took a bench in front of the Glockenspiel. Nate spread the blanket over their shoulders, and Millie snuggled up against Nate to keep warm.

"Is it always this cool this time of year?"

"No. It is unusually cool for this time of year. I am glad it is cool," he said as he put his arm around her and pulled her close. Her thoughts turned to Marion. It was assumed that once she got a divorce and was free, she could marry him. She was now unsure of everything. She liked Marion, but she knew she didn't love him. She pushed him from her thoughts.

"Nate, tell me about your wife."

"There is not much to tell. We got married very quickly after we met. She is older than me. We never spent much time together."

Why does he think that I am older than he is? Still probing she said, "Do you regret ever marrying her?"

"That is a strange question. Do you regret your marriage?"

"No, I don't. Like you I was not married very long. In many ways, it was the best thing that happened to me. In others, not so good."

"You are going to have to explain that."

"Well, I will use your words. It is complicated."

"Do you want to get back together with your husband?"

"No, maybe, I don't know." Millie was confused, and she knew what she said would make no sense to Nate. She wanted to take the conversation in a different direction. "You asked me once if I had children. Do you have children?"

Nate smiled. "No, I don't."

"You said getting a divorce was complicated. How so?"

"That is something you could never understand, so I don't think I will try to explain it to you. I have never regretted having to wait for a divorce until now." He thought of Marta. "No, that's not exactly true. I can't explain. No, that's not true either. I don't want to explain."

Nate reached down, put his hand under Millie's chin, and lifted her face toward his. He kissed her and then moved his head away, looking into her eyes. "Let me repeat. I have never regretted having to wait for a divorce until now." He didn't want to explain his relationship with Marta.

Millie smiled at Nate. *Is he falling in love with Bobbi? If he is, what happens to Millie?* She gave him a smile and quickly kissed him. "The time is just not right for us. Things are moving so fast. We have just met, and yet I feel like I have known you for a long time. Do you think we can fall in love this quickly? Maybe we are both so lonely that we are just caught up in the moment."

"Maybe so, maybe not. I will be back in the States in a few months. I could look you up. It is just a short train ride from Boston to New York." He reached into his pocket and pulled a card out of his billfold. He handed her a card. "This has my address on it. When you get back to New York, I would like for you to write to me from time to time. If you don't, I will understand."

The only thing different about me and Bobbi is the name. He likes me for me. Maybe I should tell him who I am. I wonder how he will react. Just for a moment, she could see herself living in Boston, the wife of Doctor Weber. She just let her mind drift in peaceful thoughts about what could be.

Millie was brought from her dreams when she heard Nate say, "Bobbi, are you still with us?"

"What? What did you say? My mind was a peaceful blank. I am sorry. What did you say?"

"What did I just say, or what did I say ten minutes ago? You seemed to have been somewhere else. Are you okay?"

"Yes, I am fine. It's so peaceful here, and I was thinking what it may have been like to live here during the war."

He reached down and took her by the hand. "You know, I came here at the end of the war. I have watched the place rebuild and people come back to life. At one time I thought I might just leave the army and live here."

"What about now? You said you are going back to the States. Are you going to stay there or come back here?"

"I plan to make my home in Boston. My parents and grandparents left Natalie and me well off. We have two homes in Boston, and I am going to trade Natalie's half of one of the homes to half of the other. It is too big for one person. I am not sure what I am going to do. What are your plans after your divorce?"

Her answer caught Nate off guard and by surprise. "I hope there won't be a divorce." *He is not going to understand that answer, and I am not going to explain it to him. I should not have said that.*

He remembered asking her back at the restaurant if she wanted a divorce, and her answer then had been vague. It was not vague now. *I don't understand this woman. She says she does not want a divorce and yet she likes me. Her kisses are real.*

He looked at his watch. "I need to get you back to your hotel. Do you want to do anything tomorrow?"

"Let me think about it. I might want to see more of Bavaria."

When they were standing at her hotel door, she said, "You asked me if I wanted to do something tomorrow. I do."

"What do you have in mind?"

"Surprise me."

"I will if you will trust me." He held her close and kissed her. She seemed to melt into his arms. He was more confused about where their relationship was going than ever. "I will pick you up at eleven."

The next morning, Nate walked up to Bobbi's hotel room door and was preparing to knock when he saw a note taped on the door.

I am in the hotel coffee shop, which is toward the back of the lobby.

Making his way to the coffee shop he spotted Bobbi. She was sitting at a counter with her back to him on the end stool. He walked up to her and said, "Have you had any breakfast?"

She used the counter stool to swing around and face him. "Yes, I couldn't sleep. I have been here for a while. What about you?"

"I have been up for a long time. I have eaten already." He noticed a newspaper lying on the stool next to her. It was in German. "Have you learned to read German since you came here?"

"What do you mean?"

He pointed to the newspaper on the stool.

"Oh. That was here when I arrived. I left it there because I didn't want anyone sitting next to me."

He picked up the paper and took a seat on the stool next to her. "I guess it is alright if I take this seat."

"Well, Doctor. What do you prescribe for us to do today?"

"We are going to have to play a part of the day by ear."

"What do you mean by play by ear?"

"They are predicting rain for today. Possibly heavy at times."

"You said part of the day. Does that mean you have something planned that will keep us out of the rain?"

"Do you remember last night, I asked you if you would trust me? Well, I am asking you again. Do you trust me?"

She gave Nate a smile. "I am not so sure. What is it that you have in mind that would involve me trusting you?"

"I want to take you to my house and fix you a lunch. It is not far, and I have planned a surprise."

Maybe when I am at his home, that would be a good time to tell him who I am. "I am going to trust you. You have been a perfect gentleman with me, and I guess I will trust your cooking."

When they stopped in front of his small house, Nate secured the Jeep for threatening weather.

"Nate, the sky is getting rather dark. The meteorologists are going to be right. It looks like we could get some very heavy weather."

As they go out of the jeep a few drops of rain were already falling.

As Nate began to secure the top. Millie said, "How come you have a house? I would have thought that you would have lived on a base."

"One of the perils of being an officer. For the last couple of years, I have lived like a civilian."

Once they were inside, she surveyed the layout of the house. It was not extremely large but did have a living room, a kitchen, and two bedrooms.

"Okay, you said that I had to trust you. What mysterious meal are you going to fix us?"

"Let's go into the kitchen. You take a seat at the table and let me surprise you with my cooking skills." He went to a small cooler sitting on the counter. He opened it and took out two bottles of Coke Cola. "It is not dark beer, but I think it will go well with what I am fixing for lunch. You want to drink out of the bottle, or do you prefer a glass?"

"Give me the full experience. I will drink out of the bottle. The Coke is cold. Where did you come up with the ice?"

"It was an adventure." He went to a cabinet and pulled out two iron skillets. He then started to slice up a couple of potatoes. Once the potatoes were frying, he took two patties of hamburger and started cooking them in the second skillet. A few minutes later he was putting together two hamburgers and buns. "I have onion, pickle, and tomatoes. Do you want the works?"

Millie was delighted he was going through all the trouble to create an American lunch. Smiling she said, "Hold the onions."

As they ate, he said, "One of the things I miss most about the States is the short-order restaurants. Have you been to Nathan's hot dog stand on Coney Island?"

"No, I have not."

"Gee girl, how can you live in New York and not have visited Nathan's? It is one of the greatest hotdog stands in the world. No, I think it is the best hotdog stand in the world. When I get back, that may be one of the first places I am going to visit."

I hope he does not start asking me more questions about New York. When would be a good time to tell him who I am? I should deflect the conversation to something else.

"How come you know so much about New York? You're a Boston boy."

Nathan got up from the table and said, "Do you want another Coke? I have some chocolate brownies."

"Yes, please, and only one brownie."

"You asked me a question about my knowledge of New York. My grandfather was an immigrant from here, really. When he came to America, he settled in New York and had his first business there. He met my grandmother there, and I still own some property in the New York area."

"So, you are not rich. You are very rich." *I have been living with his sister and I knew they had wealth, but they must be extremely wealthy.*

Nate cleaned up the table and said, "Let's go back in the living room. You can finish your Coke in there." They sat down on the couch together and suddenly there was a clap of thunder, and they could hear the rain coming down extremely hard. Nate got up and looked out the window. "Gosh, it is coming down. Looks like you are going to be stuck here for a while." He took his seat back on the couch.

"Thank you for going to the trouble of fixing me an American meal today. I have eaten too much. I didn't sleep well last night, and I am sleepy now. I don't think I am going to be good company."

"I have asked you to trust me several times in the past twenty-four hours. Trust me one more time. Come with me." She got up from the couch, and he took her by the hand and led her to a bedroom.

"What is going on, Nate?" She was a little concerned. She felt that he might try to make love to her, and she was not sure how she should respond. She liked him but was not going to sleep with him as Bobbi.

"I said trust me one more time." He led her to a bed and said, "Lie down and look up and just listen."

She was still unsure about what was going on, but she did as he requested, and looking up she could see the ceiling had a glass opening showing the sky, but it was obscured by the heavy rain.

"Close your eyes and just listen."

She closed her eyes, and the rain was creating a peaceful steady roar, and she didn't want to open them. Nate got a blanket, covered Millie, and lay down beside her.

"You said that you didn't sleep well last night. Let's just lie here and listen to nature's beautiful sound of rain. It may just put you to sleep."

She turned toward him, gave him a quick kiss on his lips, and said, "Thank you." She then turned her back to him and she felt him put his arm around her and pull her close. She closed her eyes and thought briefly of Rosemary's story of being with Nate in the Ardennes. In just a few minutes she drifted off to sleep.

Nate lay in the bed and could smell the perfume that Bobbi was wearing. He lay very still, and her breathing became deep, and he knew she had gone to sleep. *She is so comfortable to be with, and I love talking with her. She doesn't let me know very much about her. She never answers a question. She just follows my question with another question. I think she may still be in love with her husband. I guess it is he who wants the divorce. I wonder what type of man would not want to keep and love Bobbi forever.*

As Millie lay in Nate's bed, she found herself in a very realistic dream. *She was on a plane, and Rosemary was seated beside her. She had her eyes closed, but she could hear talking above the roar of the engines of the plane. She heard Rosemary say, "Her blood pressure has dropped to a critical point. See if the pilot can divert the plane back to London." She could hear nothing for a few minutes, then the talking started again. The pilot said, "We have passed the point of no return. We are closer to Boston than we are to London." She felt someone wiping something on her arm and then a sharp prick of a needle. She felt safe again, and in a few minutes, she heard Rosemary say, "This has bought us some time. Let's hope we can make it to Boston."*

When Millie awoke, she kept her eyes closed for a moment. She could feel that Nate was still lying beside her and knew that he had gone to sleep also. She could see a clock on the nightstand next to the bed. It was still early, and she could hear the rain still falling on the roof. She thought, That was no dream. *That was a memory. I owe my life to so many people. Tonight, I am going to tell Nate who I am and hope he will forgive me for the deception.* She shifted her weight to turn in the bed and faced Nate. She snuggled her head into his chest and thought. As she listened to the light noise coming from the rain, she drifted off to sleep a second time.

When she opened her eyes, she was face to face with Nate. He said nothing but kissed her on the lips and moved to her neck. She knew she should stop him, but she did not. He quickly removed her top and continued kissing down her neck until he was kissing the top of her breast. Reaching behind her he undid her bra and from that point on she was totally his. He was gentle in his lovemaking, and they made love several times before he brought them both to a climax. She held him tight and never wanted to let him go. "Nate," she said, "There is something I need to tell you. My name is not Bobbi Lanter. My name is Millie Berenson."

"Bobbi, are you awake? We slept all afternoon. I have had a wonderful daytime nap, but all good things must come to end."

For a moment she was confused. She was fully clothed. It was all just a dream. A wonderful dream she thought to herself. "You need to get me back to the hotel." She glanced up at the ceiling. "I can see that it has stopped raining."

Nate started to kiss Bobbi, but she pulled back. He looked at the clock. "It is early. Are you in a hurry?"

"No. I want to go back to the hotel, and change clothes into something I could walk in. I want to take a walk. The air is so fresh and smells so good after a rain. I feel it might be cool after this rain, and I might need something a little warmer. Please take me back now."

"Are you going to take this walk by yourself?" he joked.

"No, silly. I am going to take the walk with you. I want to tell you something."

"Okay. Let me brush my teeth and change my shirt, and I will be ready to go."

When they got to the hotel, Nate dropped Bobbi off in the front and said, "I am going to find a place to park, and then go in and wait for you at the hotel bar. Don't rush."

Millie got out of the Jeep and went to her room. She quickly changed into a sweater and slacks and went to the bar.

When Nate looked up and saw her, he said, "That was quick. You look nice."

"I thought that this might be a little warmer."

"Do you want something to drink?"

"No thanks. Let's walk for a while."

They walked and talked for a couple of hours and during that time Millie found she was laughing and enjoying Nate. They made their way back to the bar. They sat and talked for about an hour, and during that time Millie consumed two daiquiris. She found she was laughing and enjoying Nate. She was about to tell him who she was when he said, "I am not going to get a divorce for a while."

This caught her off-guard. "Why? You said you wanted a divorce, and I feel like you are courting me, so you need to explain to me what is going on."

"I like you very much, but when I asked you if you wanted a divorce you said, 'Yes, no, and I don't know,' and then later you said you didn't want to get a divorce. I am not sure what signals you are sending me."

Now is not the time to tell him who I am. I will wait until tomorrow. "I am not sending any signals. I like you a lot. Things are moving fast. We need a little more time to get to know who we are and what we want. Please be patient with me."

"I must work for the next three days. I enjoyed today. May I see you tomorrow night?"

Nate walked her back to her room and again took her in his arms and said, "I am looking forward to seeing you tomorrow night." His kiss was long and passionate. "I will see you tomorrow."

Millie went inside her room and lay across her bed. She started thinking about her dream where she and Nate had made love. "Why did it have to be a dream?"

The next night as she waited for Nate, she thought about just telling who she was and just seeing what happened. But she was going to see him about four or five more times, and she didn't want to spoil the time she had left with him. She would wait until she was about to leave and then tell him.

They were only able to see each other at night during the week, and they laughed, hugged, and gave each other friendly kisses. On Thursday she and Nate went to a small bar that was within walking distance of her hotel. They were seated in a booth when he said, "If I asked you to wait for me, would you?"

Now is the time to tell him. She had not expected him to ask her to wait. She didn't know what he expected. "What do you mean wait for you? You know that I am going back this weekend. I must leave Sunday. Are you asking me to wait until you come to the United States, or are you asking me to wait for your divorce?"

"I am asking you to wait until I am back in the United States. Once I am back in the United States, we could get to know each other. You can't know someone under our circumstances. I want you to know me as I would be out of the army and working in a hospital and seeing you as you live in the States. We could date while we wait for our divorces."

"Sounds like you are buying time to get a divorce. I really don't know if you are even going to get a divorce. You say it's complicated. All divorces are complicated. I am the same woman here as I would be in the United States."

Tell him, tell him now. You can bring this all to an end by simply telling him the truth.

Before she could say anything, he said, "The purpose of asking you to wait is so we can get to know each other better."

Nate is not saying that he loves Millie or Bobbi. He wants to just take a wait-and-see approach. He has had lots of time to end our marriage. Why has he waited and why is he still waiting? There must be more.

"I like you, Nate. But you have told me nothing about your divorce other than it's complicated. I want to know why your divorce is complicated. For all I know, you are trying to patch things up. I could fall in love with you, but I am not going to be the other woman." Millie knew she was pushing Nate to tell her why he had not gotten a divorce. Maybe if she knew, it would break the barriers keeping them apart. *Maybe the reason he is not getting a divorce is keeping them together. He loves Bobbi. He does not love me. If I tell him right now, will he see us as one person or two?*

Nate didn't say anything. He just sat and thought. "What if I trusted you with information that very few people know? I love my sister, and she is my best friend, and I have not shared this information even with her. I don't want to lose you. Can I trust you with my secret?"

She leaned up and kissed Nate. She felt bad. She was forcing him into something he didn't want to do. She then changed her mind. She felt she that had pushed him so far. "You don't have to tell me anything."

"I need to let you know this. It will help you understand who I am."

"Please Nate, if you have a secret you need to keep, you don't have to tell me."

"I have kept this secret for the last three years. It has disrupted my life beyond belief. It has affected my relationship with my sister, and I am sure that my wife thinks I am a cruel man for not sharing information with her."

Nate started to tell his story. "Back in 1945, I was part of the team that liberated Dachau. We thought we had moved everybody out of the dirty stalags to clean areas of the camp, and I was walking back through the camp and found a woman under a mattress. She was not in good shape. My main nurse was Rosemary Harris. Using actual mother's milk and a bottle, we stabilized her and were barely keeping her alive. She was completely covered with bedsores and bug bites. We did not have the facilities to keep her alive, so I contacted my sister, who is a doctor at Boston General, to see if they could take her into their critical care unit. She got them to agree. The problem was that there was no way to get her there. It just so happened that Senator Logan Taylor was on a committee that was gathering information about the post-war decisions that had to be made and was in Bavaria. His son had been wounded in the back, and his chances were slim. My team operated and luck was on our side. I went to see if Senator Taylor could pull some strings to get Millie, which was her name, to the Boston hospital. He felt that he owed me a favor. He did not, but we worked out an arrangement where if I married my patient, we could use the War Brides Act to bring her to the United States. Her full name was Millie Becker Berenson. That is all we knew about her. I guessed her age to be around forty-five to fifty, but it was hard to tell because of her condition. All that was good, but there was one problem. It seems that marrying a person to bring them to the United States and that is the only purpose of the marriage is against the law. Senator Taylor knew that we were breaking the law. Senator had and still has a close relationship with President Truman. He is now a powerful cabinet member. If information about this incident got out now, he might lose his cabinet post, I might end up in jail, and poor Millie would be deported. To get Millie to the United States we had to bend some rules and break others. We made a fake background check. I am sure that that background check has long since disappeared. That was a biggie. Millie had no choice about the marriage. Saving her life or not, I am not sure how she will react to all this. I held her hand and signed the marriage document. Senator Taylor and members of his trusted staff have buried most of the documents associated with this event. I said he buried them, but they are still there. So, I had to put some distance between my marriage in April of 1945 and the present. Time must pass so that when I do get a divorce no one will question the marriage. It needs to look as if we tried but just couldn't make the marriage work. Senator Taylor is powerful and may want to run for president someday. If he does decide to run for a high office, such as president or vice president, five years is enough time so these documents will not resurface."

When Nate finished his story, tears were running down Millie's eyes. "So how long does this marriage have to last?"

"Five years. Senator and I have agreed that I can't get a divorce for five years."

"You have trusted me with this information. Why don't you see your wife and trust her with the information? After all, she has a major stake in this too."

"I don't want to see her. I never want to see her. If there is some way I can pull off a divorce and never see her I will be satisfied."

"I don't understand. How could you possibly feel this way?"

"Some people, and possibly Millie Berenson, will see this as some noble act on my part. It was not. I am just a doctor, and I chose the only way I could to save my patient. I was not being noble for Millie Berenson. I was being a doctor. I don't want anybody to think I was being noble, and I especially don't want Millie to feel that she owes me anything. I was nothing more than a doctor trying to save a patient's life. I looked at the options and took the only one I had."

"So where is this pseudo wife of yours now?"

"She is in Boston. She has been living with my sister and now has an apartment of her own. She is a doctor and doing well. If I had gone back to Boston, I would have had to meet her. That would have changed everything in my life."

"So, you are never going to meet her."

"No. Can you understand how I feel?"

Millie found she was getting angry, and she didn't know why. "No. I think you are a cruel man. I don't think you are looking any further than how you feel and not thinking of how Millie Berenson feels. Can you even begin to imagine what she must be going through? According to your story, she almost dies in a prison camp and wakes up thousands of miles away in a clean hospital bed, surrounded by people who don't speak German, and is told she is married. I would guess that she has lost more than you can imagine. Did she have a family? Did she have a boyfriend or husband? Yes, I think you have given this very little thought about the consequences of the actions you have taken. You have saved her life, but you may have taken that same life from her. Does she know anything about you?"

"My sister has explained most of the situation to her. She should know there is a long list of people who helped save her, starting with Senator Taylor, my nurse, my sister, a German mother, and others. Not one of us expects her to look us up and praise us."

"What if she wants to? What if giving thanks is something she needs to do. Maybe that would give her some closure. Nate, I know you are a good man. I called you a cruel man. In a sense you are. You have made every decision about this woman and given her not even the smallest of choices."

"I knew you would not understand. I hope you understand this. Every time I see you, I want to know you better and want you to feel the same way about me. You must keep this information secret. I want you to think about what I asked you tonight. I will come by in the morning and we can discuss it more."

"Nate, I am sorry. Do you know what I heard when you told me the story of your wife? She was nothing more than a patient to you, but I am not sure she was even that. You married her to save her, and now you want to be rid of her without ever seeing her. She is also a human being. You would think a caring doctor would want one last checkup of his patient before he dismissed her into the world. There is much damage that can be done here. I would think there is much damage that is already done."

Nate could not understand why Bobbi was reacting to him that way. He had to think. Nate looked at his watch. A little over half an hour had passed. "I need to get you back to your hotel. I will be at the restaurant in the morning at nine-thirty. Think over my question and tell me tomorrow if you will give me some time. Try not to be too hard on me."

When Nate walked Millie back to her hotel room, he could feel that something was not right. He took her in his arms and said, "I know things didn't go very well tonight. I tried to be honest with you, and I don't think things came out right. I promise that in the morning I will try to make things better." He kissed her on the forehead and watched her disappear into her room without saying anything.

Nate started back down to the lobby and then turned and looked back at the door. *What in the hell just happened? I have been wrong. I should have contacted Millie and let her know who I am. No, I should have returned to Boston, checked up on her, and shared the secret of how she got into the United States. In a few months, I will be in Boston. I am going to fix all this. I will let Bobbi know and again ask her to wait for my divorce.*

Back inside her hotel room, Millie laid back on her bed. *What have I done? I need to tell him who I am. He has fallen in love with me. Has he fallen in love with me, or has he fallen in love with Bobbi? How could he fall in love with me in just a week? If I tell him who I am, how is he going to react after what he has just told me? If I leave without some type of explanation, he is going to think I am investigating him. What about me? Do I love him or am I in love with the doctor who saved me? If I am in love with just the doctor who saved me, then what Nate feared is true. If I go back to the United States, it will be at least three months before he sees me. Will his love or attraction for me be gone? If he has feelings for me, they are for Bobbi and when he finds out that I am Millie, will he still have the same feelings? He thinks I am fifty years old. How can I fix this?*

As Nate walked back to his Jeep, he tried to make some sense of what happened. *Does Bobbi have feelings for me? She called me a cruel man, but she does not know how I feel. I am proud of Millie. She has risen from the dead and become a highly successful doctor in Boston. In the morning when I see Bobbi, I am going to tell her that I am going to contact Millie and tell her who I am, and when I get to Boston, I will tell her the whole story.*

Millie did not stay in her room very long. She got up and walked down to the hotel desk. "Do you have a train schedule?"

The clerk reached into a desk drawer and pulled out several large sheets of paper. "I do. When do you want to leave, and where do you want to go?"

"I want to leave as soon as possible, and I want to go to Zurich."

"There is a train leaving in the morning at eight o'clock. You would need to be there at seven-thirty to get your ticket. I can have transportation ready to pick you up at seven. Just be in the lobby at that time."

Back in her room, Millie took a seat at the small table, took out an envelope and paper, and started to write.

She started to write Dear Nate. She wadded up the paper. *I am not going to be that informal.* She started again.

Doctor Weber,

Thank you for the last several days. During that time, you have been very kind to me, but I have not been kind to you. I have deceived you. You have no idea who I am. If you have feelings for me, you have feelings for a person who does not exist. If we should ever meet again, I would hope that you would have feelings for me, and not the person I pretended to be while I was here. I am going back to the United States to wait for my husband and hope that he will forgive me and love me for who I am. I know that last night you told me information that you want to keep private. You can rest assured that I will keep your secret safe.

Bobbi

Home

The next morning, Millie carried her luggage to the lobby. A new clerk was at the desk. "Are you Bobbi Lanter?"

"Yes."

"I was left a note about what you needed this morning. The car is not here yet. It will be just a minute. Just leave your luggage by the door, and I will see that it is loaded when your car arrives."

Millie reached into her coat pocket. "I have a letter. I think that sometime this morning, a man will come looking for me. His name is Doctor Nate Weber. Would you give him the letter? If he does not come by noon, just drop it in your outgoing mail." She handed him the letter and several bills.

"Thank you so much. I see your ride is here. I will help you with your luggage."

At nine-thirty Millie was on a train heading to Zurich, and Nate was in the café waiting for her. At ten o'clock he decided she was not coming and went to her hotel. He thought about going straight to her room but decided he should check in with the desk clerk. "Is Bobbi Lanter in her room, or do you know?"

"Miss Lanter has checked out. Are you Doctor Weber?"

"Yes."

"She left you a message." The clerk reached inside a drawer, pulled out the letter, and handed it to Nate. Nate took the letter and walked back to the café and was seated at his favorite seat. He opened the letter and read it to himself. *She is going back to her husband. I guess that is that.*

Millie wanted to go back to see her aunt and uncle but was afraid she might cause them harm. She had to change trains twice, and when she got to the Swiss border, she changed passports and started using her real identification.

She already had a ticket to London, but she would have to update the time and date. She went to a purser to have her luggage stored.

"How long will you be leaving your luggage? You will have to have a ticket to leave it here."

"I have a ticket." She quickly showed it to the agent. "I need to go to a bank here in Zurich. I don't think it will take long."

The agent quickly glanced at the ticket. "How quickly do you want to leave?"

"I don't think it will take more than a few hours to do my business at the bank."

"I can get you on a plane for London tonight. It will leave at 8:00. Is that okay?"

At the bank, she showed her key and gave her account number to a bank clerk.

He looked at the number and wrote down the balance in the account. The balance was the same as she remembered. She had hoped that it had changed and that her father had taken some of the money. *My family never had any chance,* she thought. She looked at the number. "I am going to go to my box, and take a couple of things out, and when I am finished, I am going to close out this account."

"Yes, ma'am. It will take only a few minutes."

There were several people ahead of her at the boxes, and she had to sign several cards. It had been several years since anyone had opened the box so, in addition to her key, she had to show identification.

The clerk took her information and key, and they went into the vault, opened her box, and took it to a private room. "I will leave you alone with your box, so when you are finished just let me know. I will be just outside."

The clerk glanced at his watch. There is no hurry, but if I am called away just tell whoever is posted that you are finished. "Please take your time. You may have noticed I did not use your key to open the box. This is an old key. It is still good and will identify you as the holder of the box. A couple of years ago we changed our system and box arrangement. You would be surprised how many boxes are here."

"I didn't think any of this looked familiar."

"The whole block of boxes that your box is in has been moved to this new area. If you keep your box, we will update your number. Your box is in room 9, block 7, and the number is 1918. Do want to keep your box? If you do, I will have your key updated. Your new key will have the number 9071918."

Millie looked at the number on the key in astonishment. The same number that was on her wrist. She had intended to close out the box, but when she saw the number of the box, she decided she would keep it. "I want to keep it."

"You will have to rent the box for at least five years and pay the cost upfront if you close out your account."

Millie paid the rent in cash and gave him her address in Boston. He gave her a receipt for the box and directions on keeping her information up to date. "It will take several minutes to get you a new key. Take your time with the box and I will be back shortly."

After he had left, Millie opened the box and looked inside. There was the stack of Swiss Francs on top of several papers, three diamond rings, her birth certificate, Benjamin's birth certificate, and a stack of stock certificates.

One ring was her grandmother's wedding ring. The other two she could not identify. *I wish I had my mother's ring.* She put the unknown rings back in the box and slipped her grandmother's ring on her ring finger. She smiled and thought, *I am a married woman, and my stingy husband didn't even give me a ring, and he is a millionaire.*

She took the cash, stocks, and birth certificates, and put them in her purse. She put the fake passport in the box, closed it up, and waited for the clerk.

When he returned, she said, "I hate to be a bother. I had forgotten that there was some cash in the box. I want to keep my account. There are 35,000 Swiss francs here. I want to add that to my account and change to an account that draws some interest."

Once she was at the Zurich airport and had her ticket to London, she got her luggage and checked into her flight. The time in Switzerland had taken her mind off Nate. She knew the complete story, and she knew that Nate would have to come to her. She would make sure he did. She just had to wait a couple of months.

Once Millie got to England, she decided she would take a passenger liner back to the United States. She was in luck, and she was able to get first-class passage for the next day on a liner named the Open Water. She wanted some time to think and some time to relax.

As she entered her stateroom on the Open Water, she felt guilty that she had spent so much money. *Why not,* she thought. *I have an excellent job and just discovered I have one hundred thousand dollars in Swiss francs.* She stayed mostly in her stateroom until the ship was out to sea. It was going to take eight days to get to New York. On the first day of the voyage, she sat on the deck and tried to push everything out of her mind and just relax. It was no use. She continued to think about Nate and why she didn't tell him who she was. It is okay, she thought. You will be able to fix this.

On the second day, she again got a deck lounge chair and took a seat. She had bought a book at the gift shop, and she started to read. She again looked at the cover. The book was *Tap Roots* by James Street. She turned it over and read about the book. She again started reading and soon found she could identify with the book's main character, Mona Dabney, and her family. The first three days passed very quickly.

On day four, she decided she would accept that she was the wife of Doctor Nathan Weber and take advantage of what that had to offer. She would put him in a position where he would have to confront her.

On day five, she was sitting in a small lounge that had a window view of the ocean. She was eating her lunch when a man came in and ordered his lunch and took a seat at a table close to hers. When the waiter brought the man his lunch he said, "Mr. Taylor, will there be anything else?"

For some reason, she turned to the man and said, "Are you related to former Senator Logan Taylor?"

The man put his sandwich back on his plate and said, "I am his son. Do you know my father?"

"We have never met, but he is a big part of my life. It is a long and complicated story." *There are strange forces at work here.*

"May I join you?" He did not wait for an answer. He got up from his table, picked up his food and drink, and took a seat with Millie.

Before he could say anything, a woman came into the lounge and came to their table. "He is worse. We are going to have to do something."

Logan Taylor Jr. had a worried look on his face. He turned to Millie. "I am sorry, what is your name?"

"My name is Millie."

"Millie, this is my sister, Leslie."

Leslie took a seat and said, "You need to finish and get back to the room. He is asking for you."

"Before I leave, one question. Millie, you said that our father was a big part of your life, but you had never met. Could you explain?"

Millie smiled, "You, your father, and a nurse name Rosemary Harris and I traveled together on a plane from Germany to England back in 1945."

"Don't tell me that you are the Jewish woman who was on the plane! I was already on the plane when they brought you aboard. You looked like a ..."

Millie interrupted him. "A dried-up hot dog."

"No, worse, No one thought you were going to make it. I am glad you did. I need to go check on Dad." He turned to his sister. "Have my sandwich fixed to go and send it to the room."

The two women talked for a few minutes, and a second woman came into the lounge. "Leslie, did you find Ray?"

"Yes, he has gone to the room."

The woman took a seat at the table and said, "I am Sam. I am sorry, what is your name?"

"My name is Millie, Doctor Millie Berenson. I assume you are Logan's wife."

"Yes," she replied.

Leslie spoke up. "You are a doctor. Father needs a doctor. Could you look at him?"

"The ship has a doctor. Has he seen your father?'

"The ship's doctor is not much more than a corpsman. I am not sure he knows anything. We need a real doctor."

"I am not sure what I can do, but I will be glad to take a look."

In just a few minutes Millie was entering the stateroom of Logan Taylor. His son was sitting on the bed next to him and was wiping his face with a damp cloth. Another man was doing something at a table in the room. Millie looked at the man, who was wearing a white outfit. "Are you the doctor?"

"I have had extremely limited medical training. I am out of my league. He is getting worse, much worse."

"May I use your stethoscope?"

Millie took the scope and went to his bed. She listened to his heart for several minutes and from several locations on his body. Using the ship's doctor's instruments, she took his blood pressure and temperature. "Mr. Taylor, you sure have got your body revved up. We need to slow you down a bit."

Logan Taylor looked at Millie. "Well, at least they found me a beautiful doctor, or maybe you are not a doctor at all. You are an angel."

"No, You are my angel. Let's see what we can get done." She turned to Logan Jr. and Leslie. "His heart rate is about 180 beats per minute. His blood pressure is 220 over 120. His body temperature is near 103. If we don't get all these numbers down, he will not make it through the day."

Logan Jr. asked, "What is causing this?"

"Your father has atrial fibrillation or A-fib. He has probably had it a long time, and it has gotten worse, a lot worse. I am going to let the ship's doctor take me to the pharmacy to see if they have what we need. While I am gone, keep doing what you were doing. Try to keep his temperature down. Strip down to his shorts and keep him as cool as possible. I will be back as soon as I find what we need."

When Millie returned, she had a host of different medications. The first thing she did was give him a shot. "That should slow you down a bit," she said. She took pills from four bottles. Helping Logan Taylor to a sitting position, she made sure he swallowed all four pills. She looked at her watch. "I need to repeat this in four hours." She set the bottles of pills on the table, wet a cloth with some alcohol, and began rubbing his chest.

Logan Taylor was extremely weak but said, "My gosh woman, that is cold. Could you cover me up? I feel I am naked."

Millie laughed, "Don't worry. I think I can control myself."

As sick as Logan Taylor was, he gave a weak laugh.

She then got up and pulled Leslie and Logan Jr. aside. "Now it is a matter of just wait and see. I am going to stay with him and check his vitals every half hour. You two need to take a break. I am sure you have not had much sleep. One of the pills I gave your father should help him go to sleep."

Leslie took her brother by the hand. "You go to your room and try to get some rest. I am going to stay here with Dad, and maybe I will go to sleep here."

With a laugh, Leslie said, "Do you have one of those pills you gave Dad for me? I need to relax too."

During the next several hours, Millie monitored Logan Taylor's vitals and recorded them. At the end of the first hour, there was a drop in the heart rate and a slight temperature drop. Two hours later, his heart rate was down to about 115 beats per minute, his blood pressure was 160 over 95 and his temperature was just a little over 100.

The pill Leslie had taken did its job, and she slept for about five hours before she awoke. She looked around the room and saw her brother and Millie standing near the bed of their father. She became alarmed. "How is he doing?"

"Better. It is about time to check him again. He has been asleep for a while, and he is breathing regularly. For a while, he would gasp every so often. If his numbers are okay when I do the next check, I am going to go try to get some sleep myself."

Hearing a quiet knock on the door, Leslie opened it and let Sam come in. "I am sorry I was gone so long. I fell into a deep sleep. I told Ray not to let me sleep too long, but he ignored me."

Ray came over and put his arms around his wife. "We all needed a break."

Millie looked at her watch. "It's time to do another check. Keep your fingers crossed." She checked his blood pressure, listened to his heart, and then looked at the brother and sister and smiled. "His temperature is 99. His heart rate is about 90 and his blood pressure is 138 over 91. He is going to be okay for a while. I am not going to give him another shot unless things go the other way. I gave him his medication about an hour ago, and he needs a second dose in about five hours. We are going to cut back just a little and see if we can get by twice a day. I am going to my room to clean up and then get something to eat. I am on the Ocean deck, room 88, and I will get something to eat at the lounge where we met. I plan to come back and check on Mr. Taylor in about six hours. If you need me and can't find me, have me paged."

Millie went back to the lounge where she had met the Taylors. When the waiter came to her booth, she said, "Can I still get breakfast?"

"Yes, ma'am. We serve breakfast all day. Just turn the menu over and you can see what we have to offer. If you don't see what you want, just let me know and we can do a custom order."

It was not long until Millie was having coffee, juice, two eggs, ham, potatoes, and toast. She thought of Nate and how she made fun of him for wanting a country breakfast and here she was just about having what he wanted. *I wish he were here with me,* she thought.

She had left her book in Logan Taylor's room, so she returned to the deck, found a chair, grabbed a blanket, stretched out, and went to sleep.

When Millie returned to Logan Taylor's room, she found he was sitting up in a chair and was drinking a glass of water.

"How is my favorite patient?"

He smiled. "I would think that I am your only patient unless you have turned this liner into a hospital ship. Junior tells me that we have met before. You were the Jewish girl in Bavaria. That is one interesting story that I have made a point not to tell anyone."

"How are you feeling?"

"Better than I have felt in several days. I knew my heart was beating fast, and I guess I should have gone to the doctor before boarding this ship. I guess what they say is true. Hindsight is 20/20."

"Let me check your vitals." She listened to his heart and then took his blood pressure. After she finished, she said, "Things are looking good, but I would not guarantee that things are going to stay that way. You need to have these checked twice a day for the rest of the trip."

Logan Taylor gave a sarcastic laugh. "This has not been a great trip for me. I have been in this room the entire trip. I want to get out some and enjoy the rest of the trip. I want to get dressed up and have a formal dinner. I promise I will not overeat and not have anything to drink. What do you think, Doc?"

"I don't see why not. All we must do is keep your blood pressure and heart rate under control. The A-fib is going to come and go. Chances are, you are never going to be normal again."

He then turned to his son. "Junior, call and see if they have a private dining room that we can have tonight. I would like to have dinner with my family and new friend. Do you have me on a restricted diet?"

"No. Just don't eat too much, really cut back on the salt, and don't drink any alcohol until you have been to a hospital for complete blood work and check-up.

"Man, you are tough on an old man. I forgot to ask. Are you with anyone on this trip?"

"No, it's just me. You know that I am married, but it looks like my husband abandoned me the very day he married me."

Logan looked strangely at Millie. "We are going to talk about that. You are going to be my date tonight. Let us all meet at about 7:00. Millie, Junior will come by and escort you to the dining area."

Millie went to a shopping area on the ship and purchased a dress to wear that night. She had her hair done, and when she put the dress on and looked in the mirror, she didn't see Millie, she saw Bobbi. The cocktail dress was dark blue and cut low to show some skin. *A little too daring she thought, but what the heck. There are just going to be a couple of married men there tonight.*

When Ray Taylor came to her cabin door and she opened it, all he could say was, "Wow." "Dad is going to have the best-looking date tonight. When he sees you, I think his heart rate is going to go sky high again." He then laughed.

Millie was beaming with pride. She laughed, "Thank you. You had better not say that in front of your wife. I need to ask a personal question. Where is Mrs. Logan Taylor?"

"You mean my mother. Mom died several years ago. And don't worry about the old man making passes at you. He has a girlfriend back in Washington. If he gets frisky, we will tell on him."

Everyone was joyful and full of conversation during the meal. The dining room was private and big enough to give everyone a lot of space, yet small enough to be intimate. When the meal was over, Logan Taylor ordered two bottles of champagne and proposed a toast. "I want everyone to know that I am following my doctor's orders and drinking fruit juice for this toast and announcement."

"Everyone please stand. First, I want to say that things have come full circle. I was part of a team that helped save Millie a few years back, and today she, along with my family, has saved me. Saving Millie came at a price. A young doctor married Millie and agreed to not get a divorce for five years. He had to do this to protect me and my political ambitions. Here's to that doctor. Doctor Nathen Weber." Everyone took a drink. "Please sit back down. If that doctor could see what Millie has become and how beautiful she is, he would never want a divorce."

Millie gave a weak smile. *I hope and I wish this were true.*

Logan Taylor continued to speak. "That is not how things work. I want everyone in this room to be the first to know that I am retiring from government and leaving Washington. I plan to live on the farm in Ohio. I might even get married again. The secret that I have hidden about how we got Millie to the United States can no longer hurt me. I don't want to make it public, but if it does become public it will no longer be a threat to my ambitions. Millie, it is my understanding you also paid a price because of this secret. Before this trip is over, come by and ask me any questions about what was done, and I will share my information with you. Thank you so much."

Millie got up from her seat, went to Logan Taylor, gave him a hug, and then buried her face in his chest and cried. After a moment she said, "Thank you."

The next morning Millie was having breakfast in the forward lounge when Sam Taylor came into the room. "May I join you?"

"Yes. Are you alone? Where is your husband?"

"Skeet shooting. Can you imagine?"

The waiter came to the table. "I will just have coffee." She then turned to Millie. "I had way too much to eat last night."

"Me too, but I still woke up hungry. I will check on Mr. Taylor once I get through eating."

"Millie, last night I noticed your number. It was from the prison camp, right? May I see it."

Millie extended her arm, and Sam took her hand and looked at the number. 09071918. "You know, this could be a date. It could be 9/07/1918.

I know you don't know this, but that is Ray's birthday. He was born September 7th, 1918."

"You know, that is strange. I never looked at it as a date. In fact I try not to look at it at all.

That afternoon, Millie had retrieved her book from Mr. Taylor's room and was in her lounge chair reading when she saw a shadow cross her book and chair. Looking up, she saw Logan Taylor Sr. "Millie, would you like to walk around the deck with me?"

She closed her book, got up from the deck chair, gave Logan Taylor a smile, and said, "I would love to. I am getting tired of reading, and a walk would be refreshing."

"What are you reading?"

"*Tap Roots*, by James Street. Are you familiar with it, Mr. Taylor?"

"No, I am not. I assume you and I are going to be friends, or at least I hope so. Please call me Logan."

"Okay, Logan. Let me start out as your doctor. How are you feeling today?"

"Good. I saw you while you were in Germany, and I was on the plane with you from Munich to London. There is no way I would have thought you would have lived, let alone become the success you made for yourself."

"You know I didn't do it alone. I could make a whole list of people that I owe for this life. I feel that in a way I have to pay these people back."

"You don't, but you have more than paid me for my little contribution. The reason I looked you up and asked you to take a walk with me is to better explain why I put you and Dr. Weber in a position not to get a divorce and swore everybody to secrecy. Back in 1945, I was one of the more powerful men in the Democratic Party. I had worked with FDR and Harry Truman. I made a lot of decisions based on my political career, and not what was best for me or my family. I thought Harry and the party would name me as his vice president for this year's election. As you can see, he did not. He is not doing very well in the polls and is not expected to win this year's election. Let me tell you how this involves you. I felt that I owed Dr. Weber something for saving my son. He was so determined to save you. If you are in politics, you don't please everyone. I also knew if I were chosen to be VP I would be investigated. A quick marriage, followed by divorce would look suspicious with an American marrying a German.

Five years would look normal and would also take us beyond the election of 1948. My staff and I took every precaution. We hid documents and blocked others from being accessed. To my knowledge, only one person has tried to access any of those records. Someone from New York named Bobbi Lanter. My office could find nothing else about her."

Millie smiled. "I hope the fact that Bobbi Lanter was looking into your records is not the reason you are getting out of politics."

"No. It is not. I am tired. I want to spend time with Junior and Sam. I have a girlfriend. Leslie has a boyfriend, who would have been on this trip, but he couldn't get away from his job. I believe they will soon be married. I guess I just want to be a family man."

"Good for you. You don't have to worry about Bobbi Lanter. I am Bobbi Lanter. While I was in Germany I was traveling under that name. I was not checking on you. I was trying to find out who my husband was. I now know."

"Why were you using the name Bobbi Lanter? I find that strange. Did you present yourself as Millie or Bobbi to Dr. Weber?"

"Nate, Dr. Weber, does not know that I was Millie. He still thinks he is married to an old woman."

"Millie, I still don't understand why you were using a fake name."

"While I was in Switzerland, I exposed the man who betrayed me and was the reason I was in a prison camp. Nazi hunters murdered him while I was there, and my aunt and uncle thought there might be some reprisal against me. It was for my protection."

"What are you going to do about Dr. Weber? From what you have told me, he thinks you are Bobbi Lanter."

"He is coming home to Boston at Christmas. We will settle things then."

Logan turned and faced Millie. "This trip is just about over. If we don't see you again, thank you for what you have done for me."

Millie put her arms around Logan and gave him a hug. "Thank you."

Back in the USA

When the ship docked and she was in New York, she took a room at a hotel that was in the heart of the city. She now had a plan, and the first step was to write a letter to Nate. She had to force him to confront her as Millie and forgive her as Bobbi.

Doctor Weber,

I am now back in the United States. I am sorry I left and didn't tell you goodbye and explain things better. My name is not Bobbi Lanter. I was wrong not to tell you that upfront. I hope that soon you will forgive me. While I was with you, I found out that I was very much in love with my husband. I am waiting for him to come to me and love me for who I am. I know that you were falling in love with Bobbi Lander. All I can say is I wish I were Bobbi, and we were meeting for the first time in Munich.

Ten days later she was back at her apartment, and two days after that she was back at work at Boston General.

One of the first things she did was to call Marion. She asked him to meet her after work at a local restaurant. She arrived early and ordered a drink. She had practiced what she was going to say. When he arrived, she was sitting at a table near a front window. When he walked to her table, she did not get up and he leaned over and tried to give her a hug. She did not respond, and he knew something was wrong. "How was your trip?"

"Both good and bad. I got to see my aunt and uncle. I went to Dachau and found my records. I got to meet my former neighbors, and I gained a greater understanding of what living in Germany during the war was like for both Jews and non-Jews.

The server came to the table, and he ordered a beer. "Do you want to tell me about it? I can tell by your tone that you did not find good news."

Millie continued. "I found that my mother, father, and brother all died in a concentration camp. The Americans bombed my childhood home. Our business was destroyed, and the property was sold to a large company that had built a large department store where our store stood. I found that the man that betrayed me and caused me to be in a prison camp was living in Switzerland."

"Good grief. What did you do?"

"My uncle knew of a secret organization that hunted down war criminals and reported him. They shot him on the street and burned his business and home. I had to change my name to be safe when I went into Germany."

"I can tell your trip was terrible, and I know you are glad to be home."

Millie's voice had a shade of bitterness. "Is this home? It is your home, but I really don't know if it is my home or not. During the last month, I have met several people who saved me from death. I met a young nurse who took care of me from Germany to Boston and may have saved my life on a plane. I met a young mother who was a German who provided me with mother's milk to keep me alive, even though she knew I was a Jew. I met a former senator, who risked his career to get me to Boston. And I know what you are wondering. I met an American doctor who was willing to give up a part of his life to save me and get me back to the United States".

"So, you now know who your husband is."

"I do."

Marion sat there in silence for a few moments. "Did you meet with him?"

"This is hard to explain. I did meet with him, but I never told him who I was. For reasons I can't explain, I just couldn't tell him I was his wife."

Again, Marion was silent for a while. Then he spoke. "What you are saying is that you had a chance to end your marriage and didn't."

Marion could sense that Millie was cold toward him. He did not understand why. "This still means you can get the divorce, and we can move on."

"Yes and no. I do know who my husband is, and no we cannot move on."

Marion was perplexed. "I don't understand. You just said you can get a divorce."

"I said I know who my husband is. I didn't say I could get a divorce. I took a cruise ship back from England and met the former senator Logan Taylor, and his family, and I now know my complete history from Dachau until now. There are several people who risked a lot to save me. Senator Taylor explained everything to me. Keeping the marriage, a secret was best for everyone involved."

"Are you saying you can't get a divorce, or are you saying that you will not get a divorce?"

Millie did not answer Marion's question. Her voice softened and she said, "You have been wonderful. I think the proper thing to say is that you deserve someone better than me, but that is just what someone says when they break up."

He repeated, "I don't understand. This trip was supposed to bring us closer together, not tear us apart. What happened on that trip that changed everything?"

"I found out that I admire you very much, I like you, you are fun to be with, but I am not in love with you. I will be frank. I met a man on the trip, and I now understand what love means. He was married and wanted me to wait for his divorce. He also knew I was married and waiting for a divorce. We were not intimate, but there was such a strong connection between us. I told him I would not wait, but the truth of the matter is I am going to wait for him. I hope you will forgive me."

Marion sat in silence and said nothing for several minutes. About that time a server came to the table and said, "Are you ready to order?"

Marion smiled and said, "No, I am leaving." He got up, and without saying anything to Millie, left.

The server was still standing at the table, "What about you? Do you want to order something?"

"Yes, bring me a bourbon. Make it a double."

Although Millie called Natalie to let her know she was back from Europe, she did not see Natalie at work, so that weekend she called her and asked if she and Tom could have dinner with her that Saturday. It was all set up, and that Saturday she was sitting down to a meal at a local restaurant. Millie spent the first part of the meal talking about her visit with her aunt and uncle. After the meal she got serious. "While I was with my aunt and uncle two men were murdered."

"Good grief, what happened," Tom was concerned.

She explained how Frank Christian and his father were killed and she used an assumed identity while traveling in Germany."

"While in Germany I saw Nate."

Natalie was not surprised. "I was not sure you would see him, but I thought you might. I should have known that you would. How did he react?"

"I didn't tell him who I really was, and I don't know why. I did not go looking for him. I accidentally ran into him at a restaurant. I was just in Germany trying to find information about my family. I let him think I was the woman on the fake passport."

"Why would you do that?"

"I think I wanted him to get to know me for who I am. At least, that is what I keep telling myself. But I did not do that. He got to know me as Bobbi Leah Lanter, a fake woman from New York. I liked him, and he liked the fake me. Every day I told myself I was going to tell him who I was. He asked me to wait for him until he came back to the United States."

Shifting in her seat, Natalie said, "Millie you should have told him who you were."

"Natalie, I love you, but I don't think you are the one to be giving me advice. You could have told me three years ago that Nate was my husband."

Natalie lowered her head and said in a faint voice, "I think you know why I didn't."

"I do. I know the whole story; I am sorry I said what I said."

Tom shifted and took a drink of his beer. "Nate told you he wanted you to wait for him. He wanted you to wait for what? For him to get out of the army, or until he got a divorce? If it were not so serious, this would be funny."

Millie looked at Tom. "I wish it were funny. He wanted me to wait until he got a divorce."

Natalie patted Millie on the hand. "So, he is willing to get a divorce. After over three years, he is willing to get a divorce! Good grief! He has put us through hell, and now he is willing to get a divorce! You got to be kidding me. He wants a divorce from the woman he is married to so he can court the woman to whom he is married. You are right Tom. If this were not so serious, I would be laughing my damn head off."

"No! He is not willing to get a divorce right away. He is going to wait even longer."

Natalie scoffed. "What in the hell is wrong with him? How much longer?"

Tom, seeing how upset Natalie was, said, "Natalie, let us stay calm. Perhaps there is more to the story."

A tear ran down Millie's cheek. "There is. Two more years, and I know why he is waiting. He was protecting me and protecting Senator Taylor. Seems that Mr. Taylor pushed some laws to the limit and may have broken a few."

Natalie said, "If Nate gave you information that was in confidence, he must really be serious about you."

"I don't need to tell you the whole story. You know most of it already. By a strange coincidence, I met Senator Taylor on the ship home. He has some health issues and is getting out of government. He says that Nate can now go ahead and get a divorce and that the marriage no longer has to be a secret."

"Good ole Nate, thinking about other people. I should have known, but why not share that information with us?"

"One thing I learned about Nate is that he wants no recognition for anything he has done. I could give you a whole list of wonderful things he has done in Europe, and he wants no credit for any of them."

"I still don't understand why you didn't tell him who you were."

"I know. I really goofed up. But it just didn't seem right, and I was scared. The last night we were together he told me he never wanted to see his wife. I felt hurt. I left the next day, and I didn't even tell him goodbye. Well, I did leave him a note. I even goofed up there. I had told him I was married when we first met, but my husband and I were separated."

Tom, who had said nothing for a few minutes, said in a whisper, "You told the truth."

"Tom, the problem is, I wrote my note to him in a way that makes it appear that I was going back to my husband. I told him in my note I was going back to the United States to wait for my husband. He has no way of knowing that the husband I was going to wait for was him. I am such a fool. In three months, so much could change. He could become bitter toward me during that time."

Tom said, "Why not just write to him and explain everything?"

"No. I need to see his face when we meet. I have made up my mind. I am going to wait. I have a plan. It involves both of you. I don't want Nate to know that Bobbi Lanter and Millie Berenson are the same person until we meet face to face."

"How can you do that without telling him who you are?"

"Nate told me that he never wants to meet his wife. He sees me as nothing more than a patient. He plans a divorce without ever meeting me. He has some misguided ideas that he will be made over like some kind of hero, and he does not want that. He told me that I was nothing more than a patient and he had to make a medical decision and marrying me was his only option to get me to your trauma unit. I am going to force him to come to me. Natalie, you just turned over the home left to you by your grandfather to Nate, right."

"Well, that is not completely true. He already owned half of it. He plans to live there when he comes back from Germany."

"Tell me about it. Where is it, and how big is it?"

"It is about eight miles from here. It is in a very nice neighborhood. It is big. It has six bedrooms, two bedrooms on the floor level and four bedrooms upstairs. You would just have to see it. In size, it is about the same size as our home."

"You mean to tell me that it has just been sitting there empty for the last few years?"

"No. Nate and I discussed the home when it was left to us. I think he always planned to live there, and then he got drafted. He just didn't know how long he was going to be gone. I am sure if he knew he was going to be gone so long we could have rented it. Tom and I hired a lady to live there and take care of the property. She lives in a small cottage in the back. Why this sudden interest in Nate's home?"

At first, Millie did not answer the question. "Did you know that Nate thinks that I am fifty years old? How did he come up with that?"

"I am not sure. Oh, I remember now. When Nate contacted me about bringing you to Boston General, he didn't know anything about you but your name. He guessed you were about forty-five to fifty. He said you weighed less than seventy pounds, and I guess you really did look old. He should see you now."

"He has. Now to answer your question. I want to live there for the next three months. I want him to open that door and see me. I want him to know that I did exactly what I said in the note I left him. I waited for my husband."

"How are you going to do that?"

"Tom, I want you to prepare divorce papers and send them to Nate. I want my name and his name on the documents. I want him to know that I know who he is. I want you to attach a note or whatever to say I want a settlement. Make sure he knows I want the house."

Tom gave a weak smile. "Nate will never part with that house."

"Tom, I don't want the house, but it will force him to see me there."

"There is something else. I have a safety deposit box. It belonged to my father, and he had almost a hundred thousand Swiss francs in the account and box. In addition to the money, there were some stocks, all in American companies. Can you help me find out the value of these, if any?"

"I know someone who can value them. He oversees all our investments. Bring me the stocks and I will take them to him tomorrow."

"I can get them right now. They are in the car."

The next day, Natalie and Tom took Millie to Nate's home. They introduced her to Bertha Willis, the lady who took care of things. Tom, Natalie, Bertha, and Millie took a seat at the kitchen table, where Bertha had coffee prepared. "Millie is going to move into the house."

"Has Doctor Weber sold the house?"

"No. I am going to tell you only part of the story, and Millie will tell you the rest. Millie is Doctor Weber's wife. They have been married for several years. They got married while in Europe. The rest of the story is, well it is complicated."

"Does this mean I am losing my job?"

Millie spoke up. "No, we want you to stay on. Tom has explained your duties to me. I don't see how you can take care of such a large house all by yourself."

"Well, nobody lives here, and it is easy to keep clean. There is a yard service that takes care of the yard. I pay a few bills each month, and that is about it."

Millie had noticed that when they had driven up to the house, there was a large three-car garage on the right side of the house. When they came in through the front door, there was a study to the left and a large dining room to the right. Walking past a set of steps that went upstairs, they entered a large family room with a breakfast area at the end. Doors led out to a patio which was covered. There was a master suite off to the left of the family room with a large bath and closet. The kitchen was attached to both the family and dining room. Upstairs there were four bedrooms, a bath, and a game room. "Good grief. How can a person afford a home like this?"

Tom scoffed. "Natalie, Nate, and you."

Turning to Bertha, Millie said, "I am going to be here until Christmas. *I hope even longer.* Would you consider moving into the main house until then? By then Doctor Weber will be here."

Bertha looked at Millie. *I wonder why she said Doctor Weber would be here at Christmas and not her husband.* "It is a big house, and I know it could be lonely. I will move in until then. I would be glad to help cook and do the laundry."

A week later, Millie moved in, and Bertha took a room upstairs. The first day that Millie was there, she and Bertha became friends. Bertha cooked for Millie, and Millie insisted that they eat together. Bertha had never met Nate. It was Natalie and Tom who hired and paid her. Millie liked living at Nate's house. She liked looking at the old photo books that she found there. She asked Natalie a ton of questions and tried to find out as much about the Weber family as possible.

Three days later, Millie got a call from Tom. "Millie, what time does your shift end today? I need you to see the broker that I gave your stocks to. He has called me and says he has some information about your stocks."

Late that afternoon, Tom and Millie were in the office of Jerry Rider.

They were sitting across the desk when he said, "I got some bad news, some good news, and some great news. Where do you want me to start?"

Millie wasn't expecting too much. "Let's get the bad news out of the way."

"Okay. Anon stock, you have one thousand shares. Anon went belly up."

"What does that mean?"

"I mean that the stock is worthless. They closed even before the war broke out. Had they held on they may have made some money."

Millie smiled. "What about the great news? I hope it is better."

"It is." He pushed a paper across the desk. "This stock was bought in the early '30s. You own one thousand shares. Since it was purchased, it has split three times. The company made lots of money because of the war. You now have four thousand shares. The stock is currently trading at five hundred dollars per share."

Millie didn't say anything. Then she said, "You mean that this stock is worth two million dollars."

"I do, and the other eight stocks are worth about one and a half million. You are an extraordinarily rich woman."

Millie did not know what to say. She turned to Tom. "What do I need to do with all this?"

Jerry Rider did not give Tom time to answer. "I need to help you at this point. We need to create you a portfolio. It is too much money to be just in stocks. If you let me, I will diversify your investments. At this point, you need to have about a third of your investments in stock, and about a third in secure bonds. I will convert the other third to cash and look for some property investments. Do you want some cash on hand?"

"Sounds good. Would you be able to get me about two hundred thousand cash?"

"I can. I will deduct my fee. Do you have a safety deposit box?"

"I do, but it is in a bank in Switzerland."

"You need one here. Set all this up and then get back with me."

She had fantasies about waiting for her husband to return. One afternoon Bertha came walking into the room singing *"Would you like to Swing on a Star."*

"Bertha, have you heard anything from Doctor Weber since you moved into this house?"

"You know I don't live in this house? I live in the back."

"Bertha, you know you don't live in the back anymore."

"I know, but living with you is only temporary."

"Why do you say that?"

She ignored the question. "Millie, I have always said what is on my mind. Something is just not right here. You referred to your husband as Doctor Weber. I had never heard of you until just a few days ago, and yet Ms. Natalie told me that you have been married for several years. You don't even have the same last name. Am I involved in some type of con?"

"I assure you that Doctor Weber and I are married, and yes, in a way, you are involved in some type of con. Our lives are complicated. I am going to explain everything tonight at dinner. Has Doctor Weber made any attempt to contact you since you have been taking care of this house?"

"No. He doesn't have any idea who I am. Wait a minute. A while back, a package did come. I put it in the basement. I remember it was strange because it had his return address on it but not only his address. I remember now, it had your name on it."

"Can you go get it?"

"It is big and heavy."

"How big and heavy? You were able to get it into the basement, were you not?"

"No. My nephew came by and helped me."

"Show me where it is."

Millie and Bertha went down to a finished basement. "Where did you put it?"

Bertha opened a door to a large walk-in closet and there the box sat. A cardboard box about four-feet square. Millie looked at the address. "Millie Berenson in care of Nate Weber." Millie quickly found a sharp tool and cut open the top of the box. Inside she found several photos of her family. She had to fight back the tears. As she looked at the photos, she realized that Nate had no idea that she was in several of the photos. She was so young when the photos were made. She now had photos of her mother, father, brother, and grandparents. All the photos were in old frames, and she decided she would put them in the hallway upstairs. There was also a metal box in the package. It was locked. She found a screwdriver in the workroom and forced it open. Inside there were some family records but also two deeds. One for her house and one for the store.

The next day she had the deeds photocopied along with her birth certificate and sent copies to Munich.

When Nate got the letter that Millie sent from New York, he looked at it and thought to himself. *Why is Bobbi writing me a letter? She has told me goodbye, and I assume she is with her husband.* Still, he couldn't help but have regrets. He had never felt the connection to any woman as much as Bobbi. She was like a soul mate. She must be. He had only known her for a brief period, and he had fallen in love. Yes, he had to admit it to himself. He was in love, and even though she was going back to her husband he felt that she loved him too. This he could not understand.

It was about a month and a half from Christmas, and Nate was going home. He packed up his belongings in a crate and had them shipped to his home address. He received two registered letters the same day. The first was from Logan Taylor.

> *Dear Nate,*
>
> *I hope you are doing well, and I am sorry I have not had more contact with you. I will be brief. My health is not the best, and I am getting out of government work. I am going to be the chairperson of the Taylor Foundation. This is mostly just a title. Nothing can hurt my political career anymore. Get your divorce and move on. Thank you for what you have done for me and what you have done for Millie. By the way, I have met her. She is remarkable, and this is something we both can be proud of.*
>
> *Thank You*
> *Logan*

I wonder how Mr. Taylor met Millie, he said to himself as he laid the letter down and opened the second letter, which was quite thick. It was from Tom, and again he noticed that it was formal. He first read the cover letter.

Nate,

Millie has figured out that you are her husband. She wants a divorce. I have included papers for you to sign and return to me. I have talked with Millie, and she will wait until you get to the United States to file. Just bring the papers with you. I must prepare you. She wants a settlement. The first part of the settlement should be easy. She wants the papers signed with both of you present. If you refuse, there is nothing she can do. The second request is big. For the last couple of months, Millie has been living in your home. She wants the home as part of the settlement. I am going to ask Millie to get another lawyer. You, Millie, and my wife are my family. I can't be involved. I don't think a judge would give Millie the house, but she will get something, and it will drag this out for several months if you contest this.

Tom

Nate laid the letter down and walked over to the window and looked out. "Well, I brought this on myself. Bobbi may have been right. I should have included Millie in the secret of how we got her to America. I guess saving her life was not enough. She has turned bitter toward me. But she is not going to get to my grandparents' house. She will have to be satisfied with a monetary settlement. I have enough money to give her, and she can buy her own house."

A week later, Nate arrived in Boston. He knew he could not just go to his house and move in because Millie was living there, so he took a room at a local motel. It was just a couple of weeks before Christmas, and he felt he needed to get things moving. On Sunday morning, he went down to a local restaurant, took a seat near a window, and ordered a cup of coffee. He found that he could not concentrate on reading the newspaper because his thoughts were of Bobbi. He remembered her coming to his table and how cute she was because she was struggling with the two dark beers she had had. If only, he thought, she was not married, if he were not tied up with Millie if she would have waited for him. *My only chance for happiness has slipped away.*

The next morning, Nate went to the hospital. Many of the people he had worked with before were still there, and it was like a reunion. After a few minutes, he saw his sister coming down the hallway. When she saw him, she ran to him and threw her arms around him. "It is about time. When did you get here?"

"A few days ago. I would have come by and asked for a place to stay, but I didn't need to be living with a lawyer who is representing Millie. Is she here at the hospital? I need to get this over with."

"No. She is on call. We could go see her tonight if you wish."

"No. I need to see Tom about a couple of things and then maybe I will see her. Could you have dinner with me tonight? Just you and me. I just need some time with my family, and do you realize there is only me and you now?"

"I can arrange that. Where would you like to go?"

"Is the Great Room still open? I want a steak, baked potato, and a salad."

"That does sound good."

"I will pick you up at 7:00. I will not keep you out too late. I am going to call Tom and see if I can come by his office this afternoon. I need to get things moving on this divorce."

Tom was not busy, so he and Nate sat down together. "Do you have the papers I sent you?"

"I do. Should I sign them now or in the presence of Millie?"

"I have told Millie to get another lawyer. I am advising you to do the same."

"I am not going to get a lawyer just yet. Do you know if Millie has secured a lawyer?"

"To my knowledge, she has not. The first meeting is one of arbitration." Tom smiled, "You could just give her the house and move on."

"I don't want to do that, but I think I have enough money to force the issue about the house. I know what she makes working at that hospital."

"Nate, Millie is rich. She can handle anything you throw at her."

"How is Millie rich?"

"You can take that up with her. Just go with the flow. I have a feeling everything is going to work out for both you and Millie's satisfaction."

"I wish I had that kind of faith."

When Natalie and Nate finished their meal, Nate said, "There is a really cute little girl living in Bavaria that is named for you."

"I know. Rosemary told me the whole story."

"You know that when Rosemary and I went to help Willa, that is when the whole series of events started that changed my life forever. Willa, Millie, Ray Taylor, and Logan Taylor, all happened in a row. It was like they were connected."

"Did you know that Millie has a number from the prison camp on her wrist?"

"Of course."

"Do you know the number?"

"I never thought too much about it. Is there some significance about it?'

"The number is 9071918. September 7, 1918. That is our birthday. It is also the birthday of Logan Taylor Jr. I bet if you checked, it would also be the birthday of Willa."

The next morning, he got a call from Natalie. "Nate, I have talked with Millie, and she says that she will meet with you on Saturday. It is going to be a dinner meeting. She wants all of us there around six o'clock."

"When she says all of us, does that mean you and Tom, or does it mean for me to bring a lawyer?"

"Millie wants the first meeting to be informal. She just wants to meet you, and she wants you to know who she is. She has promised that she will not make over you and act like you are some sort of god."

"She wants me to get to know her. I think I know her well enough already."

"No, Nate. You really don't. You at least owe her that. Oh, by the way. It is going to be a formal event. So, clean up."

"Good grief, I will have to buy some clothes," he said as he hung up the phone.

That week Millie received a registered letter from the government in Bavaria. It said that her case was sent to a judge in arbitration. His ruling was final. She had been awarded two hundred thousand American dollars, and a check would follow. She would still own the lot where her house stood. Once she received the check, she was to send the deed to the store property to their office.

That Saturday, Nate arrived at his home a few minutes early, and he was the first to arrive. He rang the doorbell, and he could hear someone coming to the door. He was preparing to meet Millie, but when the door opened, he was greeted by a black woman wearing an apron, and a bonnet on her head. Bertha said in a serious voice, "May I help you?"

"I am here to see Millie Berenson."

"I am sorry. You have got the wrong house. This is the home of Doctor Weber, and he is currently out of the country." She then closed the door in his face.

"What the hell." He rang the doorbell again.

This time he was greeted by the same woman, who was laughing when she said, "Doctor Weber, we have been expecting you. I was just playing a little joke. Please come in. Let's go into the family room. I have coffee on the table in front of the fireplace. Millie is getting ready. She will join you shortly."

Nate followed Bertha into the family room. Nate had forgotten how big it was. There were several chairs in a semi-circle around the fireplace.

"Please take a seat. I am doing a little cooking in the kitchen, so you just make yourself at home." Then she laughed again. "Make yourself at home. This is your home. By the way, my name is Bertha, and thanks for the raise."

"I gave you a raise?"

"You sure did. It was a nice one."

"You are welcome." Nate poured himself a cup of coffee and waited. Then he heard the doorbell ring. He shouted back to the kitchen. "I will get it, Bertha. It will be Natalie and Tom."

When Nate opened the door, there stood Tom and Natalie. Tom was wearing a black tuxedo, and Natalie was wearing a gold gown, with her hair down. "When you told me this was going to be formal, I thought that it was stupid. But seeing you two all dressed up is wonderful. Please come in."

"Nate you look absolutely fabulous. Have you met Millie yet?"

"No. She is in the bedroom getting ready. I see she has quickly become an American. She is making me wait."

When they went into the family room, Bertha stuck her head out of the kitchen and said, "Hello Natalie, Hello Tom. Make yourself at home. I got the champagne cooling, but I have apple juice for you and the baby."

"Thank you, I can't be giving my baby alcohol."

As Natalie and Tom took their seats, Nate spoke up. "Sis, I am so sorry. I have been so caught up in my own problems that I have not thought about how you and the baby are doing. Have you given the little crumb grabber a name?"

"We have. If it is a boy, we are going to name the little crumbgrabber, as you called him, Tommy Nathan Elliston. If it is a girl, we are going to name her Tommie Millie Elliston."

"Sound like a plan. I would be proud and honored for my nephew to have my name." *Millie and Natalie must have really become close. Looks like Millie is going to be a part of my life, whether I like it or not.*

Natalie stood up and gave Nate a hug. "I see you have met Bertha. You are going to love her. She is wonderful."

He gave a chuckle, "I must like her already. I gave her a raise."

The conversations were halted by the ringing of the doorbell followed by a gentle knock. Bertha yelled from the kitchen, "Can you get that Nate, my hands are full."

Nate smiled at Natalie, "I have been here only a few minutes and Bertha is trying to domesticate me." He went to the door, and to his shock there stood Rosemary and her husband. "Gosh, Rosemary, you clean up well." He gave her a long hug. "This must be Jim."

"This is Jim. I have talked about you so much; he feels like he knows you."

Jim extended his hand to Nate. "I do feel like I know you, and I am quite jealous. You have been the subject of many conversations around our house."

"I should be the one that is jealous. All Rosemary talked about while in Europe was you. Please come in."

As Nate showed Rosemary and Jim to the family room, the bell rang again. This time when he opened the door, it was Logan Taylor Jr. and his wife. Ray extended his hand and said, "Doctor Weber, do you remember me?"

"Ray, of course I do. How is that old back wound?"

"It is doing fine, and Father sends his regrets. He would have liked to have been here."

"And who is this young lady you have on your arm?"

"This is Sam, my wife."

"Doctor Weber, it is so nice to meet you, and thank you for the nice letter you sent to me after Ray's surgery."

As Nate walked back to the family room, he thought, *This is turning into something I wanted to avoid. I don't want this homecoming to be about me.*

Bertha brought out a few more chairs, and the room got loud with conversation. Then the room got quiet. Standing in the doorway was Millie. She was wearing a red off-the-shoulder evening dress that was cut low, showing some cleavage. She had on a pair of white gloves that came up past the elbows, the waist was fitted and showed off her figure. Her dark hair was piled up to one side, and she was wearing a short gold necklace.

Everyone was stunned by her beauty. The silence was broken when Natalie said, "My gosh, you look incredible."

Nate stood up and said, "Bobbi."

With both hands, Millie motioned for Nate to retake his seat. She took her finger to her lips as if to say, Don't say anything. Nate sat back down.

"I am so happy that you are all here. First, let me tell Nate that my name is Millie and not Bobbi. Let me just say, I wish I were Bobbi. The people in this room all shared a secret that you never let me in on. You all knew who my husband was. As the evidence grew that Nate was my husband, I thought I had fallen in love. I had not. I was just grateful and thankful that someone saved me, but I was not in love."

Nate was in a daze. He could not believe this was Millie and not Bobbi and she was saying she did not love him.

Millie continued, "Since I was in Dachau, good things have happened to me. I got best friends, Natalie, and Tom, I met a wonderful person in Rosemary, I got to meet Logan Taylor and Logan Taylor Jr. and his wife. I became a doctor, and I became rich. With all that, my life was not complete. It was when I went home to Bavaria that things began to fall into place. That is when I met Doctor Weber for the first time. I am so sorry, Nate, that I didn't tell you who I really was, and don't ask me to explain because I can't. All I know is that I fell in love. I didn't fall in love with my doctor, I fell in love with the man. I understand if you don't love me. We can fix that, and we both can move on."

Nate looked at Millie and said in a low voice, "We need to talk."

Millie smiled back, "I know, but not right now. For the moment, I am the host of a dinner party." She turned and walked back toward the kitchen and said, "Bertha do you need any help?"

"No, it is just about ready. Why don't you take our guests into the dining room and show them their seats?"

Place cards showed everybody their seats, and they all took their places standing behind their chairs.

Millie stood behind the chair on the end. Nate was seated at the other end of the table. "Please take your seats, and Bertha will serve the vichyssoise."

As the soup was placed in front of each guest Bertha heard someone say that the soup looked delicious. Bertha said, "Oh, I can't take credit for the… or whatever you call it. Millie made the soup."

The vichyssoise was followed by blackened chicken, with green beans and whipped potatoes. After serving the first course, Bertha took her seat at the table. The dessert was German apple cake.

After everyone finished, Millie said, "Let's wait a few minutes, and we will have the cake in the family room. I am going to help Bertha clean up the table and move the dishes back to the kitchen, and then I will join you."

It took Millie about ten minutes to get everything taken care of in the kitchen. It made little difference to the guests except for Nate. He was perplexed. The night had him completely off balance. How could Bobbi be Millie? He pulled Natalie aside and said, "How can that woman be Millie? She is far too young. She is Bobbi. Are you in on this?"

"Millie is the same age as we are. When you sent her to me, she looked incredibly old. She could have been any age. If you had lived without food for almost a year, I wonder what you would look like. As her health improved, she became the woman you see today. She is both beautiful outside and inside. I don't know what you plan to do, but you are not going to hurt her. I think all she wanted was for you to see her in a different light. Not as a patient, but as a young woman having a dinner party. If you do anything to spoil that, I will throw your ass out of Boston."

Nate paused for a moment and then he said, "That is awful strong language. I am not sure what is expected of me. I must agree. She is beautiful. She was beautiful when we met in Germany and even more beautiful now."

Nate walked away from Natalie and stood by the door. It was not long until Millie came through the door, and as she did, she did not notice Nate standing just inside. Without warning, he took her by the arm, guided her back to the office, and closed the door. Neither said anything. They just looked at each other. Then Nate spoke in a monotone. "This has been a very nice party, but I really don't know what is going on."

"I am sorry, Nate, I know I have been unfair, and I should have told you who I was back in Munich. I was scared when you told me that you never wanted to meet your wife. I have messed up. For some crazy reason, I thought if you saw me in a completely different setting... I don't know what I thought." A tear appeared in her eye and rolled down her cheek. "If you will come to Tom's office Monday, we can sign the papers and end all this. I don't want to take your house from you. Just do me a favor. Help me finish tonight and make sure everyone leaves in good spirits."

Nate walked over and faced Millie, took a handkerchief from his coat pocket, and wiped the tears from her face. "Step one on finishing tonight is not to mess up your make-up."

She smiled and said, "Thank you."

"You know that I have kissed my wife several times and didn't know who I was kissing." He placed his hand under her chin and lifted her face up toward his as to give her a kiss, then at the last minute pulled back.

She could feel that he was about to kiss her but did not. "What is step two," she asked. She put her arms around him and laid her head over on his chest.

"Step two is getting rid of all these people so we can talk. I want to talk about that divorce, and see what we need to do about that." He then took her by the hand and led her back to the family room. She had some concerns but also felt some relief.

When Natalie saw them re-enter the room and that they were holding hands, she felt relieved. She could tell things were going okay. No one else even seemed to notice that they had even left the room.

Bertha came into the room carrying a pot of coffee. "Everyone grab a cup. I have already cut the cake, and it is on the counter." Millie came over and gave Bertha a hug. "Thank you. Don't you leave. You are a working guest. I sure appreciate what you have done."

Millie motioned Bertha to join her in the kitchen. "I am sorry I left you alone. I will help you get things cleaned up so you can join us in the family room."

"There is not much left to do. Natalie has been helping, and just about everything is taken care of except what we are using now. Get a piece of cake, and enjoy your own dessert. I have already taken a taste, and it is delicious."

The rest of the night went well, and about ten o'clock, Natalie and Tom were the first to leave, followed by Rosemary and Jim. Before they left, Nate took Millie aside, and said, "Don't you think we should ask Rosemary and Jim to stay here?"

"I have already asked them, and they want to use this trip as a second honeymoon. They are staying at my apartment and are going to visit the city before they go back to Maine."

Once everyone was gone, Millie said to Nate, "I am going to slip into something a bit more comfortable. Make yourself at home until I return, and then we will talk. That sounds strange telling you to make yourself at home in your own home."

"Bertha said the same thing."

Millie went to her bedroom, took off her evening clothes, and put on a pair of loose-fitting white pants and a black pullover shirt. She let her hair down and brushed out the kinks. When she returned, she was surprised to see that Nate had also changed clothes. He was wearing a pair of brown slacks, and a light blue sweatshirt. "Where did those clothes come from," she said.

"I came prepared. I hate wearing formal clothing. You look comfortable."

Millie noticed that the room had been rearranged back to its normal arrangement. Nate noticed that she had seen the change and said, "Bertha helped me move things back. I like the couch in front of the fireplace."

"Where is Bertha?"

About that time Bertha came into the room. "Bertha is right here, but Bertha is leaving. I have had a great time being a part of this. I have called my nephew to come and pick me up. I am going to spend the rest of the weekend with my sister. I see his lights are outside right now. I will be back Tuesday morning. You two are adults, and you don't need supervision."

After Bertha was gone, Millie and Nate sat on the couch and for a few minutes said nothing. Nate broke the silence. "You know that in some ways I feel like we are strangers, and in other ways, I feel like I have known you forever. I don't know how to say this in any other way but to just say it. I thought I was falling in love with Bobbi, but I was falling in love with Millie. I really don't know who you are. I know this sounds crazy, but every time I look at you, I see Bobbi. Who were you when we were together in Bavaria?"

This was not the type of conversation that Millie had expected. She answered very slowly. "I came to Munich to find out what happened to my family. I ran into you by mere chance at the diner. I was not even sure I would meet you while I was there. I was not Bobbi in Bavaria. I was a very confused Millie."

"You said that you can't explain why you didn't tell me who you were? So why were you using the name Bobbi?"

"You don't know what happened to me before I was in Dachau. A friend betrayed me. When I came back to Switzerland, I reported him to my uncle, who reported him and his father to the underground. They killed him and his father. My aunt and uncle were afraid that some retribution might come to me. They helped me change my name while I was in Germany for my protection. So, I will just echo what you said back. I was falling in love with Doctor Weber while I was there. I was not falling in love with my husband. I don't know how we can fix all this unless you can accept me as Millie, and I can forget that you are the doctor who saved my life."

As they sat on the couch, they said nothing for a while, and Nate started to think about the fact that he had been cruel. He had looked after her wounds and starving body but had not really thought too much about what she had gone through. If her mind had healed, it was not his doing. Some of the credit belonged to his sister. She had healed her and taken her into her home, but most of the credit belonged to Millie herself.

Breaking the silence Millie said in a soft low voice, "What are you going to do now that you are back in the United States."

"Not sure. There is a research hospital here in Boston. I might go talk to them, but I also have a project about which I am thinking. I guess you are going to stay at Boston General."

"Not sure. There is a place in Switzerland that is taking displaced children from Germany. I understand they need a doctor that speaks German. I am going to investigate that. Are we both avoiding what we know we must discuss? What are we going to do? I still have my apartment. I am going to move back there and let you have your house. I never planned to stay here."

Nate took a deep breath. "You wanted to make this marriage work."

Millie gave Nate a weak smile. "You said it. Nate and Bobbi might make a go at it, but Nate and Millie will not. I am not two people. I am Millie. Bobbi was a name change. Nothing more."

Nate didn't say anything for a moment. "I need to get to really know you, Millie. It seems so strange that I see you as two people. You are not going anywhere. You are going to stay in this house for a while. We are not getting a divorce until I know who I am divorcing. Walk me to the door. I will pick you up at noon tomorrow for lunch. I want to revisit the city, and I want you with me."

When they reached the door, Nate put on his coat and turned and faced Millie. He put his arms around her and said, "Forgive me. I have not been a good husband. Let's pretend it was our first date and we are saying good night." He pulled her close and kissed her, and when he broke off the kiss, she did not want to let him go.

"I will pick you up at noon tomorrow."

"Don't leave. Stay with me." She took him by the hand and pulled him away from the door. "Don't leave. I want you to stay."

Nate took off his coat, pitched it on the floor, took her in his arms, and kissed her. "Are you sure this is what you want?"

She gave him a nervous look and said, "Give me a moment." She gave him a quick kiss and quickly disappeared down the hall toward her room.

As he watched her leave, he reached down and picked up his coat. He thought he should leave. *There is no turning back if you stay,* he thought to himself. He walked back into the family room. *Maybe I don't want to turn back. Millie, Bobbi, what difference does it make? They are one and the same.*

He didn't have to wait long, and Millie came into the room wearing a blue housecoat. "You look nice," he said.

"I was afraid you might leave."

"I have to be honest, I thought about it. But this is what I want." He put his hands on her waist and again kissed her. When they broke this kiss, she took him by the hand and led him to her bedroom. The room was dark except for the light of a candle which flickered and gave the room an amber glow.

She released his hand and walked over to the window that overlooked the backyard. She opened the curtains and looked out. "It is beginning to snow. I love snow. It makes everything pure and white, and everything dirty disappears."

Nate walked over and put his arms around her, and they both looked out the window. Then he kissed her on the back of the neck, untied the housecoat, pulled it from her shoulders, and let it drop to the floor. She was wearing a light blue negligee. He turned her to face him, and one of the thin straps fell from her shoulder. *This woman is a goddess.* He again kissed her and as he did, he noticed that she was trembling. "Are you scared of me?"

"No. I am excited. No, that's not true. I am excited and scared. Please be patient with me. I want this," and she reached down to his waist and pulled the sweatshirt up and over his head. She kissed him on the chest and then laid her head on him. He could feel her breast pressing against him. He reached down, picked her up, and laid her on the bed. He removed his pants and lay down beside her. She was still trembling, and he could tell she had never been with a man before. He really wanted to take her, but he knew he must be gentle. He propped himself up on one elbow and just looked at her.

She turned toward him, "What are you doing?"

"I am just looking at you. You have to be the most beautiful woman I have ever seen." He reached over and pulled the negligee up and she helped him remove it. He kissed her again and as he did, he let his hands explore her body. She could feel his excitement, and she was no longer nervous. Trembling was replaced with extreme passion. Pain was replaced with pleasure, and their bodies molded together.

The next morning, there was enough light coming through the window to light the room. Millie had her back to Nate, and he had his arm around her. She moved just a little and when she did, he said, "Good morning."

She turned to face him and gave him a smile. Pulling the sheet up to cover her body, she smiled and said, "I am sorry, I have never done this before?"

"I know," he said.

"How could you know that I have never slept in the nude before?"

He laughed, gave her a kiss, and said, "I am starving. I hope you have some breakfast food here."

"Nope, just leftovers from last night."

Nate pushed back the covers of the bed, got up, and walked over to the window. It had only snowed a little. "Hop up. We will get something to eat."

She laughed. "You might feel comfortable walking around in the nude, but I don't. Get your clothes and get out of here."

He came to the bed, grabbed the covers, pulled them from the bed, and then jumped in bed beside her. He pulled her to him. "Breakfast can wait."

It was near ten-thirty before they were ready to leave to find something to eat. As Nate slipped on his coat he said, "I hope we can find a place still serving breakfast."

"It is Sunday morning. I think most restaurants will be serving a late breakfast."

"I wonder if Marty's is still open."

When they pulled into Marty's, there was only a moderate crowd, and they were quickly seated. As they looked at the menu, coffee and water were brought to the table.

Laying the menu down for a minute Nate said, "What are you going to have?"

"I think I will have a waffle. The one with a fruit topping."

Nate looked up at the waitress. "Bring my wife" and he stressed the word wife, "a waffle with fruit topping, and I will have two eggs over medium, sausage, potatoes, and a side of biscuits and gravy."

"Good grief, Nate. You surely can't eat all that. Is this that southern breakfast you talked about in Germany?"

"It is, and I have looked forward to this for the past four years."

Eating slowly, they talked during the meal. Finally, Nate pushed back his plate and said, "This is all I can hold. I am done. It was great."

"Well, you ate most of it. Nate, what do we need to do next? Last night was wonderful, but it does not obligate you to me."

"I feel differently. I hope that last night was a commitment. We are married, but we were never truly married. I want us to get married again. It doesn't have to be anything big, but it needs to be nice and formal. I don't have a lot of friends, but I would like to have the ones that I do have witness my commitment to this marriage."

"So, when we leave here, we need to go by your motel room and pick up your belongings. You will need to get a job. You are going to have to support me, you know."

"Tom said you had money. Don't you know I am marrying you for your wealth?" He laughed. "Tom didn't say how much money you had only he said you were rich. I guess Natalie has already told you, oh how do you say it? We are loaded. Neither of us must work, but I want to."

Millie pushed her plate toward the center of the table and said, "I will have to go to the hospital tomorrow. What are you going to do? You know you are somewhat famous, and I am sure you could get a job there. Natalie is going to be taking maternity leave on the first of the year. You might take her place until she comes back."

"Let me think about it. If I do this, it would only be temporary. I was thinking about starting a clinic for children who were injured during the war. I am going to contact Logan Taylor, and see if this is something his foundation would be interested in co-sponsoring." Getting up from the table, he said, "I am going to go pay the bill."

While Nate was at the counter, Millie noticed a piano in the corner. She walked over and took a seat on the piano bench and started to play. She was surprised at how easily it came to her. Nate looked at her playing and smiled. When she finished, he said, "You never cease to amaze me. You play well."

"I have not played since I left Switzerland, and I didn't play much while I was going to school there.

"You need to take it up again. You have some real skills."

"I know you went to my childhood home. Did you see our piano there?"

"I went through your home and got your photos and some other things, but I never saw a piano."

Millie had a sad look on her face. "I went there too, but I didn't go in. Our piano was a Blüthner. It was extremely old and had the most incredible sound. I wish I still had it. I had no desire to ever play again until now."

On Christmas Eve, Millie was working at the hospital and Nate had bought a Blüthner piano as a Christmas gift. It was placed next to the Christmas tree.

When Millie came in that night, she saw it and started to cry. "It looks just like the one we had when I was growing up." She sat down and started to play. As she played, tears rolled down her cheeks. "I don't deserve all this."

Nate sat down next to her on the piano bench. "Don't be silly. You have paid an extremely high price for what you now have."

That night as they lay in bed, Millie snuggled up against Nate. He pulled her close. "I have talked to Logan. His foundation is going to co-sponsor our clinic. We could have everything set up by summer. We can expect about forty young refugees before the summer's end."

"That's wonderful," she said, as she drifted off to sleep. She closed her eyes and thought of the day she spent at Nate's house in Munich. She remembered her dream. She stretched up and kissed Nate on the forehead and thought to herself, *This is better than a dream.*

Printed in the United States
by Baker & Taylor Publisher Services